The Lost Queen

Sharon C. Jenkins

First Edition published by Sharon C. Jenkins 2023

Copyright © 2023 by Sharon C. Jenkins

All rights reserved. No part of this publication may be reproduced, stored, or transmitted in any form or by any means, electronic, mechanical, photocopying, recording, scanning, or otherwise without written permission from the publisher. It is illegal to copy this book, post it to a website, or distribute it by any other means without permission.

This novel is entirely a work of fiction. The names, characters and incidents portrayed in it are the work of the author's imagination. Any resemblance to actual persons, living or dead, events or localities is entirely coincidental.

Sharon C. Jenkins asserts the moral right to be identified as the author of this work.

First Edition
Editing by Jason E. Jenkins Editing by Brianna Sanchez Editing by Beautifully Edited, LLC

This novella is a tribute to the courageous women who have embraced the divine power of God and found strength in moments of vulnerability.

Continue on, my sisters, continue on...

The tremendous support from my incredible community of fellow writers made The Lost Queen a reality.

I am deeply grateful to the following individuals:

Walda Collins (Marine), author of A Warrior's Sword, 10 Strategies to Build Hope and Stand Strong in the Midst of a Battle. Her book provided essential spiritual insights that influenced this novel.

Kenneth Andrus (Navy), whose valuable input helped shape any scenes involving watercraft, drones, and rescuing damsels in distress on the high seas.

Marcus P. Griffin (Air Force) is an expert in crafting captivating heroines with impeccable attention to detail. His expertise was instrumental in editing this book.

Lila Holley (Army), and The Camouflaged Sisters for their invaluable assistance throughout the process.

Jason E. Jenkins (Army), demonstrated unwavering support during editing and overall production, a true testament to his love for the project.

TABLE OF CONTENTS

INTRODUCTION

Prologue

The sweet fragrance of honeysuckle permeated the air as the turtledoves sang a lovely seductive chorus. Their high-pitched coo could be heard throughout the garden by anyone who was in listening distance. But the two young lovers seated on a marble bench seemed oblivious to their symphony. On the left was a stately young gentleman with piercing blue topaz eyes and hair the color of a blond palomino. Opposite him sat a slender, exquisite masterpiece of a woman that rivaled the masterpieces of Amy Sherald… and they were entwined in an intimate conversation that would redden the face of any Catholic priest. After all, they were betrothed, by no consequence of their own, but destiny had brought them together again and now they were inseparable.

Previously bound by a contract signed in front of the archbishop and everyone who was anybody in the dynasty. It may have been mere writing on a piece of paper, but it was so much more because it bound them together in ways that superseded their imagination. She was his and he was hers forever… At least until that fateful day in her office.

The Broken Covenant

After what some would say was a lover's spat, she tore up that contract and bid him farewell to his motherland after she was slapped in the face with his arrogance. She loved him then, but her duty to her country and his American ways were butting into each other. He disrespected her in front of the high council, and he had to go. When he left that day, he took a part of her heart with him. But she had to send him away because his actions could have cost her the dynasty. Her people needed her… especially after the untimely murder of her father, Oba Jaiye. From the time she was a little girl, she'd been groomed to be a royal. There had not been a day of her life when she wasn't aware of who she was and what that would require of her. That's why it was so obvious what course of action she must take to save face and her royal family's name. If her father were still alive, he would have been beheaded. In the days following, she told herself that she had spared his life by her actions. But as the days got shorter and the nights got longer, she realized that she had a hidden motive for her actions. He had not chosen her; her father chose him for her. It was uncharacteristic for her to be rebellious, but she was tired of being a pawn on a royal chessboard. Her own father had laid in her arms and declared her "a waste of good seed".

All because he wanted a male heir. She had been the best daughter possible to him and he rewarded her with his disdain. All the men that she had loved or attempted to love had required her to be something that served their purpose. Her father wanted her to rule his dynasty the way he would rule it, even though she was not his first choice. Sarki, the man who murdered her father wanted her to be his wife so that he could be king someday, and now Ezra Jr. demanding that she continue their courtship during one of the busiest times in the dynasty. NO! She would not be a pawn in another man's hand. She deserved to be loved, respected, and honored. She would wait. If love happened it happened, but when it did it would be on her terms. She was a good catch, and her man would need to recognize that and act accordingly.

Meanwhile, in America, Ezra Jr., or E., as he is more commonly known, was lost in a ball of confusion. He ran to his mother's home like a scorned suitor, hoping that she could help him figure it out. He asked her a million times, why had Zara sent him home. Eventually, she told him that they both were grown, and they would have to work this out on their own. He was so furious that he went to his room and didn't talk to her for days.

Did Zara even love him? If she did. Why did she send him away? They were still bound by the contract to continue their courtship. That was until she tore it up. The dying wish of her father was that he take care of her in his absence. Had she forgotten that? He couldn't do that as her betrothed. He literally had no power to do anything for her in a foreign country where he had yet to become a citizen. Couldn't she see that? He was looking out for her best interest, and she tore up the agreement and sent him home. Now who would protect her? Women! Several weeks went by with no word from Zara or anybody from the Dala Dynasty. The only thing he got from the dynasty was a certified letter requesting his banking information. Now she wanted to pay him off for time spent in the courtship. Well, she could keep her money, he didn't want it. He wanted her. The realization hit him like a load of bricks one day when he was working out. He'd heard that exercise was good for depression, and he started using his kid brother' s weights to keep his mind and body preoccupied, but he couldn't use them 24 /7. Sweat was dripping from every crevice of his body, but he still put additional weights on the dumbbell and tried to exorcise the very thought of loving Zara from his mind. He approached his mom again and she told him to "talk to the hand", and quickly exited his room.

On the day that he thought he couldn't take it anymore, he heard from his father who was still in the Dala Dynasty. He agreed to be an advocate for him with Zara but didn't offer much hope. He chastised his son for his impatience and shook his head at his youthful ignorance as he hastily tried to tell him his side of the story.

It took his father three weeks to get to see Zara. When he did, she was polite, but unyielding regarding his son. That was until he asked her if she loved E. That's when the concrete walls came tumbling down. He noticed her eyes watering and soon regretted asking the question. She was quick with her answer.

"Yes, I love E. but I will no longer allow myself to be ruled by my emotions". Zara sat up in her chair and eyeballed Ezra Sr.

"I want a man to love me with the romantic love that seemed to escape the understanding of my father. He must choose me above all else. In my case, he would need to be comfortable with being second in command because I will not give up my throne for anyone".

"What about being a wife to this man Zara? How would you manage that and rule the Dala Dynasty?"

"I have thought about that. I would rule the dynasty and he would rule everything connected to us as a family. He would be the head of our household and manage the palace compound, the stables, our finances, and me of course".

"I see. In other words, he would be the neck that holds the head in place".

"Yes. That's what I envision the role of my husband to be". The telephone rang and Zara picked up the receiver. "Yes. Thank you for reminding me. Tell the chief that I look forward to our meeting and that I will meet with him shortly". She turned to the Chancellor, "Thank you so much for checking on me. I genuinely appreciate it and look forward to us having dinner sometime soon".

"Zara, I am leaving for America tomorrow. It's been a while since I've been home".

As she walked him to the door she said, "Please tell everyone I send my love". She tiptoed and kissed him on the cheek. "Safe travels Uncle".

He smiled at her saying, "I will be back in a month. Sooner, if you need me. I am only a telephone call away. Odaabo Zara".

"Odaabo".

The Decision

Call it ego or pride, it didn't matter, E. was struggling with it regularly. In addition, his younger brother was pranking him. He figured it was because he wanted his room back.

He was fed up with this whole situation with Zara. She had sent a check to his mother's house and he tore it up the moment he recognized it for what it was. Originally, he'd thought Zara had come to her senses and finally sent him a letter of apology, but to his disappointment, it was a check. His mother and stepdad just stood there staring at him like he had lost his mind. Later that day they talked about having him committed or having some kind of intervention. They both were shocked when he suddenly appeared at the door with a duffle bag thrown over his shoulders. Immediately the telephone rang. His mother picked it up.

"Hello? Oh hi, Ezra. Yes, he's here. Sure. It's your father he wants to speak with you".

"Dad?"

"Son, I don't have a lot of time, because I've got a plane to catch. So, I'm going to give it to you straight. There is trouble in the dynasty. It appears as though there is going to be a civil war. Zara's in trouble and she needs us. Now. If you love her, you better be at the airfield in one hour".

"Who would do something like that?"

"That's not important right now, Zara is. If you're not there in an hour, son, you might be missing out on the one chance in a lifetime to get it right. Don't do what I did with your mother. I let my pride get in the way and I lost the only woman that I 've ever loved. Don't let history repeat itself. Bye".

"Dad?"

E. stood there looking at the phone for a second.

Julie asked, "What's the matter son? Is your father alright?"

"Yes ma'am. But Zara's not, her country is about to go to war?"

"What?"

He reached out and pulled his mom into his arms saying, "I love you".

"I love you too. Do I need to ask where you are going?"

"No ma'am".

"You love her don't you?" "Yes".

" I thought so. I 'll be praying for you and your dad, son".

"Thank you, Mom. I 'll definitely need it".

The Rescue

When E. And his father arrived in the Dala Dynasty, Zara was headed to the battlefield. E. was in a peculiar situation because of his having been exiled by the queen. He found favor with the head of the Palace Compound's security team and was allowed to go to the battlefield where Zara was leading her troops into battle. A long-haired more muscular version of E. rode up on her late father's Black Stallion; steely blue eyes focused on the object of his desire.

Nafisa, the head of the queen's security team shouted, "Ni irorun!" The Alagbatas' spears were placed back in their sheaths. E. asked Nafisa if he could approach the queen. She looked directly at Zara, and she nodded her approval. He maneuvered his horse with expert skill to land directly beside the queen. She looked at him, giving him a consummate professional response. "I understand you have a message for me of great importance".

He obstinately replied with heartfelt conviction. "I refuse to let the woman I love go into battle without being by her side. I remember a time when you shared these words with me in one of our Bible studies from the Book of Ruth, 'Do not press me to leave you or to turn back from following you! Where you go, I will go; Where you lodge, I will lodge; your people shall be my people, and your God my God. Where you die, I will die… there will I be buried.'"

E. dismounted from his horse and bowed down on one knee, saying: I make this same pledge to you my Royal Highness. Initially, I came at the request of your father, but today I come because my heart won't let me do anything else but love you".

Queen Zara led her troops into a victorious battle that day. The history books would later call it the Battle of Shike Hill. The unfortunate consequence was that Ropo escaped, which did little to damper the queen's enthusiasm. On the last day of the battle, E. got on his knees again and asked the queen to marry him. The entire camp cheered when she said, "Yes".

CHAPTER 1

*L*ingering on thoughts of love would not solve the problems of the dynasty. Zara was like a pubescent schoolgirl after sneaking a morning kiss from E. on the way to her first meeting of the day. Her schedule was packed, as usual, and she needed to adjust her crown before her day progressed.

Sneaking around with her beloved was further complicated by the constant coverage of her security team, the Alagbatas. They were fierce women warriors with combat skills that rivaled the best soldiers in the Dala Dynasty's secret military forces. Their names were: Aarifa, Fazilah, Hiba, Leila, Nafisa, Tiwa and Yaya.

Nafisa was their commander-in-chief. The only time she could escape them was when Queen Zara went to the bathroom. So the young lovers identified bathrooms that were near where she was going to be during the day, and she would slip into their secret meeting place and find him waiting there in one of the stalls. No one was allowed to enter the restroom when she had to go, so it was the perfect meeting place. Except for the one time that she was drastically late because of a hearing, and he had to climb out of the window to escape bumping into the janitor who arrived before the queen to tidy up. That evening at dinner they laughed so hard that they both were bowed over in pain before they could stop.

Zara often found herself in the middle of the night wondering if an extended courtship was the best course of action for them. They had been through more in their betrothal period than most couples went through during their marriage. E. was being patient, but she also knew his reason for doing so… he didn't want to lose her again.

Queen Zara Akinyemi of the Dala Dynasty was a good queen. If it hadn't been for her age and the discord that Sarki's father, Ropo Achempong had sown in the dynasty, she would have been highly respected by all of her subjects. The untimely death of her father had thrust her on the throne long before she anticipated. She was grateful for his insistence on her preparation for the crown from the time she was a toddler until now, but she would give anything for him to still be alive. Reminiscing about the recent darkness of the murders of her father and Sarki, the former head of security who once was a childhood friend would do her no good. She couldn't change the course of their histories if she wanted to. Her solace for the immense grief she'd felt was often found in the pages of the Bible, her Iya had given her. When

E. was in the West; she'd given up any hope of reconciliation and threw herself into running the dynasty as a way to escape it all. It was easy to do, being a queen was a 24-hour job. She was surrounded by excellent advisors, her military leadership had faith in her as commander-in-chief. Ezra Sr., her soon-to-be father-in-law had taken an active role as Chancellor in assisting her in running the country by being a goodwill ambassador solidifying relations with their allies. The Dala Dynasty was on its way to recovery after a tumultuous year. At least, that's what she thought.

The Ominous Full Moon

The queen of the dynasty had falsely believed that darkness was gone, unaware that it was merely hiding, waiting for its opportunity to strike again. It seemed fitting that on this dark luminous night, the only light came from a mysterious full moon, casting an eerie glow on the path leading to the queen's door. The figure approaching her door moved silently and with labored breaths, occasionally emitting a sinister whimper as evidence of the many injuries endured over time - wounds sustained by a loyal body determined to serve without faltering.

It was midnight and someone was ferociously knocking on the door of the king's mansion which now housed everyone in the royal family and their support staff. Ezra Sr. happened to be getting a bedtime snack when he heard the pounding. He was hesitant to open the door because whoever it was had bypassed security and made it to the rear of the compound where his dear friend Oba Jaiye once lived. When no one immediately answered the door, he had no choice but to respond. The incessant noise was hideously loud and threatened to wake up the entire household. He grabbed one of the swords off of the wall and answered the door. An older Nigerian woman was chattering in Yoruba standing in front of him. She saw the sword in his hand and fell to the ground. It was then that he noticed that her feet were bloody. He rushed over to the wall and pulled the security alarm. Immediately Vincent, the head of palace security, and Nafisa, the head of the queen' s security were at the door with guns drawn. The woman remained prostrate on the floor with a look of horror on her face. Vincent was the first to inquire about their mysterious visitor.

"Who is this woman?"

"I have no idea", Ezra Sr. replied.

Vincent turned towards the woman and asked in Yoruba: "Tani"

The woman responded in her native tongue, "I am from Alimosho. I am here to warn the queen that Ropo and his men are on their way to burn down the palace compound and assassinate the Royal Highness".

Vincent exclaimed, "Olorun mi"

He continued his interrogation, "How do you know this?"

She responded. "I work in the house of my master as a maid. I heard him talking with Ropo about his plans to overthrow the government. I came to warn the queen. She has shown great kindness to my family".

He looked at Nafisa, "Do you believe her?

"Yes, it appears that she has come a long way and suffered much to get here", she responds looking at her scarred feet and legs.

"Can you tell me when the attack will take place?" he asked.

"Tomorrow", the older woman responded.

"Do you know how many men he has with him?," Vincent replied.

"Hundreds", she said.

Ezra Sr. who had been quiet up to now, asked, "What's going on?"

Vincent shook his head and responded, "I am afraid the queen's life is in danger. We will have to move her quickly". He looked at Nafsa and said, "Implement Code Red immediately. Considering the distance between her village and the compound, Ropo may be here sooner than we think. We can't take any chances. Prepare the queen for travel immediately".

E. suddenly appeared in the foyer. Witnessing the scene, he asked, "Is there a problem?"

His father responded, "The palace compound will be attacked within the next 24 hours. We have to get Zara out of here before they get here".

"She won't go", he replied.

Vincent shouted, "Yes she will, even if I have to drag her out of the compound myself". E. questionably looked at his father who said, "Son, I think the best course of action is to remove the queen. She can't run the dynasty dead".

The reality of his father's statement hit him in the gut. He'd never heard Vincent shout in the entire time he'd known him. This was a lot more serious than he thought.

"Gentlemen let' s continue this conversation in the study", Vincent said, gesturing towards the study door.

The two men followed Vincent as he went to a bookshelf and pulled out a book titled *War and Peace.* The bookcase had a Murphy door that opened slowly and behind it was a hidden room. Vincent walked into the closet-sized room and opened a metal cabinet with one of the keys on a chain that was hidden in his jacket. He pulled out an envelope marked "For Emergencies Only". Ezra noticed that the instructions were written in the handwriting of his boyhood friend Oba Jaiye. When

Vincent shook the envelope, two small brass keys fell into his hand. He looked at both men standing before him and said, "When I insert this key in that lock, pointing to a switch enclosed in a glass case, "we will have 60 minutes to leave the premises. According to these instructions I only have ten minutes to turn on the switch once the door is opened. That doesn't leave us much time. I advise you to go gather your things and meet me in the foyer in 20 minutes.

E. asked, "What about Zara?"

Vincent replied, "She's already gone".

Both Johnson men looked at each other in utter shock.

"I advise you to get a move on it if we are going to join her".

When the men passed through the foyer, on the way to their rooms, they noticed that the old woman was no longer there, the floor was spotless. Matter of fact, if they didn't know any better, they would have thought it was all a bad dream.

The Queen Disappears

Zara was startled awake by the thundering sound of horse hooves on a dusty path. Just three hours earlier, she had been peacefully saying her nighttime prayers, ready to embark on a journey into dreamland. Settling her head onto the soft satin pillow, Zara anticipated dreams of an attractive man with long blonde hair tied in a ponytail. In no time at all, she was drifting off into a tranquil night filled with exciting escapades.

Now it appeared that she was an unwilling passenger on an unplanned journey to God knows where. She tried to talk, but she had a splitting headache. What in the world was happening? The only thing she immediately recognized was that they were headed toward a nearby body of water. But it could be the Red Sea, the Atlantic Ocean, the Indian Ocean, or the Mediterranean Sea. Had she been kidnapped? How in the world did that occur? She had some of the best security in the world. It had to have been an inside job. But who would want to betray her? Just then the bad headache began to pound and she let out a whimper.

Lelia shouted to Nafisa, " I think she's awake". Nafisa hesitated and reluctantly addressed the queen. "Your Royal Highness, are you awake?" Zara mumbled, "I am. Where are we and why are we here?" she mumbled.

"Your Royal Highness, I have some unfortunate bad news to share with you".

"What is it?"

"The palace compound has been seized". "What? That's insane…"

"It appears that Ropo was able to rebuild his army and we were notified that he was on his way to take over the palace compound".

"Is that why I 'm being kidnapped?"

"No, Your Highness. You are being rescued".

"Now you know better Nafisa. Turn me back around right now!

"I can't your Royal Highness".

"Why is that? Do you defy a direct order from your queen?"

"No, Your Highness. We are just following the instructions of the head of security, Vincent".

Zara moaned. "He is not the queen!"

"No, your Royal Highness, but when this is a Code Red situation. His primary mission is to get you to safety and his mission has become our mission".

This information sobered Zara. "So where are you taking me?"

"We don't know all the details, but your father left explicit instructions that you be removed from the compound".

"My father? My father is dead!"

"Yes, Your Highness, but he left explicit instructions for Vincent if a situation of this nature ever occurred".

"How in the world can a dead man rule from the grave?"

There was complete silence.

"Why wasn't I awakened when this happened?"

"We don't know Your Highness. Our instructions have always been in a Code Red situation to get you to a safe place by any means necessary".

"By any means necessary… what… did you drug me?"

Again there was complete silence.

"I asked you a question, Nafisa! Did you drug me?"

"Yes Your Highness, I did".

Zara screamed at the top of her lungs. Once she finished, she looked at the trembling figure on the horse next to her and said, "You are no longer commander-in-chief of my security team. I will appoint someone else as soon as I get rid of this splitting headache".

"Yes, Your Royal Highness".

Nafisa turned her head back towards their destination, extremely grateful that she was going to get to live another day.

The Wall (Ogiri Naa)

They left the compound with ten minutes to spare. E., Vincent, and Ezra Sr. were in the lead Range Rover, headed towards the private airstrip traveling at a rate of speed that would defy most of the speed limits in several countries combined when the ground began to tremble. The caravan came to a sudden stop, each man tumbled out of their vehicles struggling to determine what caused such a horrendous shaking of the earth. They were fifty men strong in twenty bulletproof SUVs including the Queen Zara look-alike.

As suddenly as it started, it stopped. The trembling ceased and when the dust settled, there was a huge metal wall that had sprung up out of nowhere surrounding the palace compound. Ezra Sr. said, "What the hell is that?" Vincent looked at him and smiled, "It's as much of a mystery to me as it is to you, but it looks like the King is living up to his word that no one would ever penetrate the walls of the Palace Compound". He chuckled and signaled for the men to resume their journey.

All of the men including two of Vincent's top security officers got back into the SUV. Each man grappled with the reality that the Compound was now a fortress of steel. Several miles down the road, E. said, "I 've seen a lot of things in my lifetime, but never anything like this. It must have taken centuries to build something like that".

"Probably not. From the looks of it, the wall was built before the compound was built". Vincent responded.

Ezra Sr. pulled off his glasses for cleaning, he stated, "Then that means it was built way before Oba Jaiye was even born. I can't believe his father had the technology to create something so ominous. Amazing!" Shaking his head in astonishment, he returned his glasses to their proper resting place.

Vincent's tablet received a notification, alerting him of a new email. He excused himself from the conversation. The Johnsons quietly contemplated the wonder that they had just witnessed. After several minutes they heard a "Holy Cow!" coming from the front of the SUV.

"I just got the update on the wall. You guys are simply not going to believe this", stated Vincent. "Here's what it says… The Dala Dynasty's defensive perimeter features a state-of-the-art impenetrable metal wall, composed of reinforced alloy panels designed to withstand extreme force and resist any attempted breaches. Equipped with advanced surveillance technology and automated defense systems, the wall acts as a formidable barrier, ensuring the city's security by thwarting any potential threats.

The impenetrable metal wall is ingeniously stored underground within a secure storage facility. When inactive, the wall's modular components are neatly arranged in a concealed chamber beneath the city's surface.

Upon detecting a potential threat, a sophisticated automated system triggers the rapid deployment of the wall, seamlessly assembling it to safeguard the city from any impending attacks.

The impenetrable metal wall is designed with integrated access points and control rooms strategically placed throughout its structure. These access points serve as entryways for a small team of highly trained soldiers responsible for monitoring and maintaining the wall's defensive systems. Equipped with living quarters, communication hubs, and surveillance stations, these fortified sections within the wall allow the team to operate efficiently and respond swiftly to any emerging threats, ensuring the city's security around the clock".

"Well Gentlemen, it appears as though Oba Jaiye's ancestors thought of everything", Ezra said.

"Indeed they did", stated E. "Now where in the world is Zara?"

A Boat Ride Like None Other

The serene calming of the sea belied the rapid beating of the young queen's heart. She was yet again under the thumb of her father, and she sincerely regretted his interference. The waves were gently hitting the shore as the seven women disembarked from their horses. Fatigued, weary, and famished, six sets of eyes looked at Nafisa.

"What? I am no longer your leader. Please consult the queen on our next step, "and she bowed before Zara with the humbleness of a royal dignitary.

Zara rubbing her head stepped away from the women contemplating their future and decided to rescind her earlier statement. She returned to the small crowd of women.

"Nafisa, because we serve a God of second chances, I will be as benevolent as he is and give you a second chance. But keep in mind, if you ever defy me again, you won't live to see the next day. Am I clear?"

"Yes, Your Highness. Thank you so much", Nafisa replied.

"Now what's next on our agenda? the queen asked.

"We are to wait here for a boat", Nafisa said. "A boat? What kind of boat?" Zara inquired.

Nafisa dutifully responded, "I don't know Your Highness. But it will be arriving within the next half hour".

Zara turned on her heels with a grunt attempting to sit down on the sand like a pouting toddler, but not before six anxious warriors rushed to put their cloaks underneath her. She scoffed at their feeble attempt to shield her bottom. After momentarily contemplating the scenario, a giggle ceremoniously popped up and out of her perfectly full contoured lips. It's infectious and pretty soon all of the women warriors were rolling around in the sand in fits of hilarious rebuttal.

The British captain of *The Bloody Hangman* stumbled upon them in disbelief. He had difficulty comprehending what lay before him. It had been years since he'd witnessed something as enticing as the last *Girl Mud Fight* he attended during his time in Cuba. He was intrigued.

And then he saw her…

Envision a young African queen, in her early twenties, reclining gracefully on a bed of military cloaks scattered across the golden sand. Her untamed beauty and allure captivate the Captain, transcending societal expectations. Adorned with intricate traditional jewelry that told the stories of her people, she embodied a perfect blend of heritage and modernity.

Her attire, a fusion of cultural garments and contemporary elements, symbolized a harmonious coexistence of tradition and progress. The warm sun accentuated the natural richness of her skin, casting a radiant glow that reflected both her individuality, and the strength rooted in her cultural background.

With confidence in her posture and a magnetic gaze fixed on him, she emanated a sense of empowerment and poise. This African queen, surrounded by the echoes of history and the embrace of nature, stands as a testament to the beauty found in authenticity and self-assurance.

He might just keep her for himself!

CHAPTER 2

Under the scorching North African sun, the vast desert landscape stretched out as far as the eye could see, its golden sands radiating heat waves that distorted the horizon. The intense midday sun beat down on the arid terrain, creating a shimmering mirage in the distance. Against this backdrop, a lone figure approached, mounted on a sleek, powerful, thoroughbred horse.

The spy, dressed in a lightweight desert-colored cloak to blend with the surroundings, urged the horse forward with swift and purposeful gestures. The horse, its coat glistening with sweat from the exertion, responded with a burst of speed, its hooves kicking up fine grains of sand as it raced across the desolate landscape.

As the spy neared the makeshift command post, the commanding officer, stationed beneath a makeshift tent to shield against the unforgiving sun, squinted to identify the rapidly approaching figure. The rhythmic galloping of hooves grew louder, resonating through the stillness of the desert.

With a cloud of dust trailing behind them, the spy and the thoroughbred reached the command post. The horse skidded to a stop, kicking up more sand as it came to a halt. He dismounting with practiced ease, and swiftly approached the commanding officer.

Beads of sweat trickled down his forehead as he delivered urgent intelligence calmly and efficiently. Ropo, acknowledging the gravity of the information, nodded solemnly. The spy stood sheepishly awaiting his next command. His commanding officer turned to the other men in the tent and said, "We have a new development, the palace compound has suddenly been surrounded by a wall that appears to be made out of metal".

A junior officer from the back of the room asked the obvious, "How are we going to get into the compound then?"

"What would you do to a wall that stands in the way of your future?" Ropo questioned him.

"Attempt to climb it", replied the young officer.

"What an astute answer…" Ropo responds. He turns to the young man saying, "And that's exactly what you will do when we arrive at the compound today. I have the utmost confidence in your ability to accomplish this task because it will cost you your life if you don't. Does anyone else have any advice to offer before we leave?"

The room was deadly silent. "I thought so", Ropo replied.

Ropo and his troops arrived at the compound in the dead heat of the day. What once was a vibrant city full of people going about their everyday lives, was now a ghost town. The only witnesses to the travesty that was about to take place were the battalion of soldiers which consisted of mercenaries, fellow tribesmen, and prisoners from the dynasty prison.

On that day, a total of one hundred individuals lost their lives while attempting to scale the impervious metallic barrier, including the youthful military officer. They departed to lay

their fallen comrades to rest, only to return the following day armed with sufficient weaponry capable of obliterating a small nation. Yet despite their efforts, the wall remained unharmed and resolute, its untainted facade serving as a constant reminder of yesterday's massacre.

Come midnight, Ropo found himself momentarily defeated as he hung his head low. He collapsed onto the ground in an unrestrained display of grief for his deceased son. "Somehow Sarki, I will avenge your untimely death or I will surely die trying".

Wrong Ship Right Direction

Queen Zara and her entourage were very grateful for the early rescue. Captain Reynold Christian was slightly overweight but otherwise in good shape. He was short with fair skin, blonde hair, and green eyes. He leads the way to the ship's gangway like a proud papa.

The modern covert vessel, sleek and cutting-edge, blended seamlessly into the busy maritime traffic. From a distance, it masqueraded as an ordinary fishing trawler, its hull painted in weathered tones to mimic the appearance of a well-worn workhorse of the sea. Closer inspection, however, would reveal the high-tech features concealed beneath the facade.

The ship's exterior was adorned with retractable nets and crates, creating an illusion of a legitimate fishing operation. Its mast carried satellite communication and radar equipment cleverly disguised as fishing gear, enabling the pirates to stay connected while maintaining the ruse. Beneath the surface, the hull boasted an advanced sonar and radar systems, allowing the vessel to navigate treacherous waters with ease and evade detection.

The crew donned outfits reminiscent of professional fishermen and moved with a purpose that transcended the ordinary. Each member was not just a pirate but a highly trained mercenary, chosen for their expertise in modern naval warfare and electronic warfare capabilities. Their appearance, though ordinary, concealed a collective proficiency in handling state-of-the-art weaponry and technology.

When the ship cruised through international waters, its seemingly sluggish pace belied the powerful engines hidden below deck. These engines, capable of rapid acceleration and high-speed maneuvers, could transform the vessel from a harmless fishing boat into a swift and elusive predator when the need arose.

Concealed within specially designed compartments were advanced weapons systems, including precision-guided missiles, an automatic cannon, and advanced automatic firearms. The pirates, each equipped with communication devices and tactical gear, maintained a constant vigil, blending in with the mundane activities of fishing while remaining ready to transition into a combat-ready state at a moment's notice.

This marauder, disguised as a fishing trawler, operated on the fringes of legality, taking advantage of its inconspicuous appearance to navigate through international waters with impunity. It was a floating fortress of technology and ruthless expertise, poised to engage in covert operations, whether it be intercepting valuable cargo or defending against threats from rival factions or law enforcement.

Unbeknownst to Queen Zara, she was walking into harm's way. The allure of their expedition had even captivated the Algabatas, who were typically in control in the forests of Africa, but novices when it came to conquering the sea. It wasn't until they were safely onboard that Captain Christian exposed his true intentions. With a beguiling smile, he announced that they were now his captives and he couldn't decide whether to keep them for his harem or sell them to the highest bidder. The Algabatas assumed a protective circle around their queen, but it was too late…every member of the crew had his weapon drawn and aimed at them.

The queen was caught off guard. She was about to signal for an attack, when Nafisa shook her head "no", and nodded towards the sky. Slightly up above them was an MQ-9 Reaper and an EMP drone. Within minutes every electronic device on the boat would be disarmed. On the horizon was a British Navy Destroyer racing toward the pirate vessel.

Captain Christian was agitated, issuing orders to his crew readying his vessel for a rapid getaway. The moment one of the sailors began to comply with his instruction, the MQ-9 Reaper commenced firing warning shots. Nafisa and Leilah swiftly moved the queen out of harm's way while the remaining Algabatas members ensured the safety of their surroundings.

The destroyer arrived shortly after, and the pirate ship's crew attempted to launch their lifeboat in vain into the water to avoid arrest. Queen Zara mumbled a prayer of gratitude.

Captain Christian made one last valiant attempt to defend his ship when he realized its electrical system was disabled. He reluctantly waved the white flag in total surrender.

When the captain of the frigate was taking the handcuffed Christian to the brig, he looked at Queen Zara and exclaimed, "Who the h_ are you anyway?" The senior officer from the recusing British vessel tightened his cuffs and he responded with a menacing groan. The officer chuckled and punctuated his actions with the following statement: "Show some respect for the Royal Highness, is that any way to talk to the Queen of the Dala Dynasty? Welcome aboard Ma'am!"

Home Sweet Home

The sun dipped below the horizon, casting hues of orange and pink across the sky, a private royal airplane descended gracefully towards the tarmac at a private terminal at an American airport. This Gulfstream G800, adorned with regal insignias, bore the unmistakable aura of royalty. Its polished exterior reflected the last rays of daylight, giving it an almost ethereal glow.

The aircraft's engines emitted a low, powerful hum as it taxied toward an exclusive landing area. The lack of the queen on board added an air of mystery to the arrival, as the absence of the royal figurehead defied expectations. Instead of the customary grandeur associated with such landings, the atmosphere was tinged with curiosity and speculation.

Uniformed airport personnel awaited the plane's arrival, their expressions a mix of professionalism and intrigue. A red carpet was rolled out, symbolizing the customary welcome for dignitaries, but the absence of a queen to grace it left an unusual void.

Her presence was usually the focal point of such arrivals, raised questions, and fueled speculation about the purpose of the visit.

Security personnel surrounded the aircraft, their presence underscoring the importance of the guests on board. A sense of anticipation lingered in the air as onlookers, both airport staff and curious bystanders, craned their necks to catch a glimpse of who might emerge from the luxurious royal airplane.

The door of the aircraft descended with a smooth mechanical whir, revealing a delegation of officials and attendants. Vincent, the Johnsons, and their military attachés debarked on the tarmac with heavy hearts.

The events of the following evening left them void of emotion and distant. Each man locked in his own interpretation of what the future of the Dala Dynasty would look like in the days to come.

The lack of a royal figurehead, however, added an enigmatic quality to the arrival, leaving observers to wonder about the reasons behind the visit and the unfolding events that would follow on American soil.

Once the gentlemen were in secured vehicles, E. asked a series of enigmatic questions, "Where is Zara?

Has anyone heard from her? Are we sure she got out of the country safely?

Vincent turned around in the front passenger seat to address his questions. "I am checking with everyone assigned to her entourage now. I should have a complete update within the hour".

E. responded, "I don't know if I can wait that long. It's been over 24 hours, and we've heard absolutely nothing. If I don't hear something by then, I'm getting on the next plane leaving for Africa to look for her".

Reaching out to touch E.'s clutched hand, Ezra Sr. comforts his son saying, "Now son, we have to let Oba Jaiye's plan run its course. It's worked so far. Give it a little bit more time. Vincent is as anxious as we are to get Zara to safety. We can do more for her from here than there anyway. Remember this is our home court". He looked at Vincent, "… that being said, what is our next step?"

"We need to find a secure place to set up a command center".

"What about my boardroom?"

"No. That's too public. Do either of you own a home?"

Both men shook their heads "No." Ezra followed up with, "But this is Houston, we can purchase one". He reached into his pocket, pulled out a cellphone and started calling local realtors.

"What can I do?" E. asked.

"It's a great time for prayer", Vincent responded.

E. acknowledged his request and bowed his head.

Two hours later three limos pulled up to a gated community on Lake Livingston. This secure hideaway was in a distinct little town called Onalaska, Texas, away from the hustle and bustle of fast-paced Houston freeways and the hurried lifestyle of city folk to a rural oasis.

This covert sanctuary was a clandestine retreat nestled within the serenity of nearly two acres of prime lakefront property. This hidden gem, a bespoke haven veiled in secrecy, unfolded as a custom-designed, resort-style refuge—an architectural masterpiece meticulously crafted with unparalleled attention to detail. As you stepped into this world of hidden allure, the sweeping open water views captivated you, setting the stage for a narrative of suspense and romance. More than a mere dwelling, this secluded abode was a backdrop where passion and mystery intertwined, promising an experience beyond the ordinary. Dining took on a discreet charm, a dance of intrigue beneath the moonlit sky, facilitated by an expansive outdoor kitchen designed for hosting confidential gatherings.

The spacious deck transformed into a covert meeting ground, offering ample space for encounters draped in secrecy, while the covered patio provided shade for discreet conversations on sunlit days. Picture stolen moments by the outdoor fireplace, where crackling flames echoed the clandestine heartbeat of hidden connections. Amidst the natural beauty, covert meals were prepared, guests were entertained with an artful finesse, and secret rendezvous were relished against a backdrop of awe-inspiring water views.

The infinity swimming pool, with its beguiling sun shelf, beckoned you to linger, inviting stolen moments of intimacy amidst the reflective waters. Inside, the expansive kitchen and living areas wove a tapestry of luxury, functionality, and stunning aesthetics—a setting where intrigue and romance found their perfect convergence. This extraordinary lakefront sanctuary transcended mere property; it was a refuge, a secret haven for those seeking solace, love, and an escape from the tumultuous world outside. Ezra Sr. seized the opportunity to claim ownership of this clandestine sanctuary, where romance and suspense would merge harmoniously against the tranquil backdrop of the lake.

When E.'s father gave him the keys to the property he said, "This is an early wedding present. Zara's coming home soon son, and you two are going to make this house a true home". Filled with overwhelming emotion, E. held his father close and cried tears of relief and happiness. At that moment, all the fear and uncertainty he had felt during his separation from Zara disappeared. With renewed hope, he could now imagine a future where he would live happily alongside her - their love as resilient as the many challenges they had faced together.

Somewhere in the distance, a lanky tween was gazing in awe at all of the commotion. The house had been emptied for months, and now as if out of an NCIS television series a limo and several black Range Rovers had pulled up in front of the house. He grabbed his fishing gear and wondered what his mother would say when he returned without their dinner.

The Lost Queen Finds a Home

Ten days later, after a journey filled with anticipation and trepidation, the British frigate finally arrived at its destination - the vast expanse of the Gulf of Mexico. As the sailors prepared to bid farewell to the queen and her entourage, a sense of melancholy settled over them. They had grown accustomed to the presence of royalty, finding solace in the familiarity of their surroundings. Yet, they knew that their mission was not to escort Zara to a life of luxury and comfort, but rather to assist her in her quest to reclaim the throne.

Despite the relative comfort of the frigate compared to the perilous conditions of a pirate ship, Zara couldn't help but feel a sense of longing for her homeland. The journey had brought her physically closer to her goal, but emotionally, she felt further away than ever. The Dala Dynasty, with all its traditions and history, seemed like a distant memory, fading with each passing day.

As the frigate docked in the United States, Zara felt a mixture of excitement and apprehension. The vastness of the country seemed to mirror the vastness of the challenges that lay ahead. Boarding a helicopter, she couldn't help but wonder where her uncertain destination would lead her. It was far from the ideal situation, but at least she was alive, defying the odds of her exile. She was extremely grateful to God for his protection, but she was going to need much more than that to resume her role as the queen of her beloved country. It was clearly evident that she was going to need a miracle!

The helicopter soared through the sky, carrying Zara further away from the familiar and into the unknown. The wind whipped through her hair, a constant reminder of the freedom she sought. The landscape below transformed from the vastness of the ocean to the sprawling cities and endless fields of the United States. It was a stark contrast to the opulence and grandeur of her former life, but Zara knew that she had to adapt and embrace this new chapter.

As the helicopter touched down, Zara took a deep breath, steeling herself for the challenges that awaited her. She was determined to reclaim her throne, to restore the glory of the Dala Dynasty. The journey had been long and arduous, but it had only strengthened her resolve. She was ready to face whatever lay ahead, armed with the memories of her homeland and the support of those who believed in her cause.

And so, Zara stepped out of the helicopter, her eyes fixed on the horizon. The journey may have taken her far from the comforts of her past, but it had also brought her closer to her destiny. With each step she took, she felt a renewed sense of purpose, a fire burning within her. The exile may have stripped her of her title, but it had also ignited a fierce determination to reclaim what was rightfully hers.

As she embarked on this new chapter of her life, Zara couldn't help but feel a sense of appreciation for the frigate and its crew. They had been her companions, her protectors, and her confidants throughout this tumultuous journey. Their unwavering support had given her strength when she needed it most. And as she looked back at the frigate one last time, she knew that she would carry their memories with her, a reminder of the resilience and camaraderie that had sustained her. Zara turned her gaze forward, ready to face the challenges that awaited her. The journey may have been long and arduous, but it had also been transformative. She had come a long way from the comforts of her former life, but she was determined to reclaim her throne and restore the glory of the Dala Dynasty. The exile had tested her in ways she never thought possible, but it had also revealed her true strength and resilience. As she took her first steps on American soil, Zara knew that she was ready to embrace her destiny and forge a new path forward, and she wouldn't have to do it alone… she had E.

CHAPTER 3

hat used to be a family room, a space for relaxation and bonding was quickly transformed into the nerve center for Vincent and the Dala Dynasty's secret service. This room, which had once been a cozy haven, now bore little resemblance to its former self. It had undergone a complete metamorphosis, becoming the epicenter of their operations, where plans were meticulously devised, intelligence was diligently gathered, and missions were expertly coordinated. It now served as the headquarters for this clandestine organization, a hub of activity and strategic thinking.

In the short time since its inception, the Secret Service team had achieved remarkable feats. They had strategically positioned their highly skilled operatives in critical geographical locations within the dynasty, ensuring that they had eyes and ears in all the right places. These agents, who possessed a unique set of talents and expertise, were deployed to key areas where they conducted covert operations and gathered vital intelligence for the Dala Dynasty. Their tireless efforts and unwavering commitment had yielded significant results.

Their diligent work had not been in vain, as they were able to identify the villages that remained loyal to the queen, as well as the key revolutionists on Ropo Achempong's team. This knowledge proved invaluable, allowing Vincent and his team to navigate the complex political landscape with precision and foresight. By understanding the allegiances and motivations of different factions, they were able to make informed decisions and take calculated actions that would shape the future of the dynasty.

The secret service team operated tirelessly, working in twelve-hour shifts to ensure round-the-clock surveillance and readiness. Their dedication and commitment were unwavering, as they fully grasped the gravity of their mission and the profound impact it could have on the future of the dynasty. They knew that their vigilance and meticulousness were paramount to the success of their covert operations.

In the early hours of the morning, around 3:00 a.m. Central Standard Time, a notification arrived, alerting the Secret Service that the Queen and her security team would be arriving by helicopter at 6:00 a.m. that very morning. This information sent ripples of anticipation through the headquarters, as the team prepared for the imminent arrival of the monarch. Every detail was meticulously planned and executed, leaving no room for error. The team's collective focus and attention to detail were palpable, as they understood the significance of this moment and the critical role they played in ensuring the safety and security of the Queen.

The Arrival

The silencing of the swirling of the helicopter blades announced their arrival at the designated destination, marking the beginning of a new day as the sun made its appearance on the horizon. Queen Zara, filled with gratitude for their safe journey, offered a quick prayer of thanksgiving, expressing her heartfelt appreciation for the pilot's skill and attentiveness throughout the flight. The pilot, ever attentive to the needs of his esteemed passenger, promptly approached Queen Zara, ready to assist her in any way necessary. Queen Zara warmly acknowledged his kindness with a heartfelt thank you, recognizing and valuing his unwavering support during their time in the air.

As she gracefully stepped out of the helicopter, Queen Zara was greeted by the breathtaking serenity of a beautifully calm and perfectly transparent freshwater lake. The tranquility of the surroundings captivated her, and for a moment, she wished she could spend the entire day immersed in this peaceful oasis, allowing the beauty of nature to wash over her and rejuvenate her spirit. However, duty called, and she knew she had a country to lead and protect, a responsibility she took with utmost seriousness and dedication.

The Algabatas, loyal companions accompanying Queen Zara on her journey, were equally mesmerized by the natural beauty that enveloped them. They took their time, savoring every moment, basking in the loveliness that surrounded them. The allure of the lake's pristine waters and the tranquility it exuded left an indelible impression on their hearts, reminding them of the importance of finding solace in nature's embrace amidst the demands of their noble duties.

Before Queen Zara could make her way to the house, the object of her affection, E., met her halfway, his presence filling her heart with joy and anticipation. Disregarding everyone and everything around them, he swept her up in his arms, a gesture of pure love and adoration that spoke volumes about the depth of their connection. The pilot, concerned about protocol and the appropriate decorum, stepped forward to intervene, but Nafisa, a trusted confidante and friend, understanding the profound love shared between Queen Zara and E., pulled him back, assuring him that E. was indeed Queen Zara's betrothed, their union blessed by the highest authority.

With a sudden halt, E. gently placed Queen Zara back on the ground, their eyes locked in a passionate gaze that conveyed a multitude of emotions. In that moment, it was as if their lives depended on the intensity of their kiss, a testament to the profound love they shared and the unbreakable bond that held them together. The world seemed to fade away as they embraced, their hearts beating in perfect harmony, their love radiating like a beacon of light in the enchanting surroundings. The beauty of the natural landscape mirrored the beauty of their love, creating a magical moment that would forever be etched in their memories, a cherished memory to draw strength from in times of adversity.

As they finally broke apart, Queen Zara and E. exchanged a knowing smile, their love stronger than ever, fortified by the challenges they had overcome and the unwavering commitment they held for each other. With a sense of purpose and determination, they continued their journey towards the house, hand in hand, ready to face whatever challenges awaited them, knowing that together they were invincible. The Algabatas followed closely behind, their hearts filled with hope and anticipation for the future of their beloved queen and her betrothed, their unwavering support a testament to the loyalty and dedication they held for their sovereign. As they approached the house, Queen Zara and E. couldn't help but feel a surge of excitement and nervousness. The suspense of what lay ahead filled their every step with a sense of adventure and possibility. They knew that within those walls, their love would be celebrated and their future would unfold, forever intertwined in a destiny that was meant to be.

But these moments of respite and relief were short-lived, as Vincent, the trusted advisor, approached them with an urgent update on the current state of affairs within the Dala Dynasty and the ongoing revolt. The queen, fully aware of the gravity of the situation, was immediately drawn into the heart of the chaos, known as Ground Zero. It was there, amidst the turmoil and uncertainty, that she dedicated the remainder of her day, with E. faithfully by her side, offering his unwavering support and counsel whenever she sought it.

Time seemed to blur as the queen navigated the treacherous waters of leadership, her mind consumed by the weight of her responsibilities. She tirelessly analyzed the intricate web of alliances and rivalries, seeking the best course of action to restore stability and order. The weight of the crown pressed upon her brow, a constant reminder of the immense burden she carried.

However, her relentless dedication did not go unnoticed, as Ezra Sr., the father of her soon-to-be husband, entered the room. With a mix of concern and affection, he gently urged the queen to take a much-needed break, insisting that she cleanse herself with a refreshing shower and find solace in a few hours of rest.

His words resonated with her, reminding her of the importance of self-care amidst the chaos.

Reluctantly, the queen acquiesced to Ezra Sr.'s well-intentioned request. She recognized the wisdom in his words and understood that she needed to recharge her weary body and mind. With a heavy sigh, she allowed herself to be guided to a new room, within the confines of a new house that she had yet to fully explore. The unfamiliar surroundings intrigued her, offering a temporary escape from the relentless demands of her role.

As she settled into the embrace of the soft covers and fresh sheets, exhaustion washed over her, lulling her into a deep and peaceful slumber. The rhythmic sound of her breath filled the room, creating a soothing melody that drowned out the noise of the outside world. In this unfamiliar sanctuary, she found a momentary respite from the chaos that awaited her in the days to come. The weight of her responsibilities momentarily lifted, allowing her to find solace in the simple act of surrendering to sleep.

In her dreams, she found herself transported to a tranquil garden, where vibrant flowers bloomed and gentle breezes whispered secrets of hope and resilience. The worries and anxieties that had plagued her waking hours melted away, replaced by a sense of serenity and tranquility. The queen reveled in this moment of respite, allowing herself to fully embrace the peace that enveloped her.

But even in her dreams, the queen's mind remained vigilant, her subconscious working tirelessly to find solutions to the challenges that lay ahead. Ideas and strategies floated through her thoughts, weaving together like a tapestry of possibilities. In this ethereal realm, she found clarity and inspiration, her mind unburdened by the constraints of reality.

As the sun began to rise, casting a warm glow over the garden, the queen reluctantly emerged from her dreamlike state. She knew that she couldn't stay in this sanctuary forever, that the world outside awaited her return. With a renewed sense of purpose and determination, she rose from the bed, ready to face the challenges that lay ahead.

The queen stepped back into the chaos, her mind fortified by the brief escape she had experienced. She knew that the road ahead would be difficult, filled with obstacles and uncertainties. But armed with the strength she had found in her moments of rest; she was ready to lead her people with unwavering resolve and unwavering support from those who stood by her side.

The Pursuit of Revenge

Ropo, consumed by an unwavering desire for retribution over the tragic loss of his beloved son, was resolute in his belief that the Queen, the perpetrator of this heinous crime, was concealed within the impenetrable fortress that once stood as the majestic palace compound. Despite his relentless efforts to infiltrate the fortified walls, his endeavors proved to be in vain, leaving him vulnerable to the merciless mockery of the tabloids. However, amidst the disheartening ridicule, Ropo found solace in the unanticipated support he received from unexpected quarters, a testament to the unwavering faith these individuals had in his noble cause. And let the tabloids revel in that revelation!

As he pondered his next course of action, Ropo convened a crucial meeting with a select group of trusted advisors, seeking their counsel and wisdom. It was during this gathering that an audacious suggestion emerged from one of his advisors, proposing the disruption of the compound's electrical power supply. Ropo swiftly admonished the individual for their ignorance, reminding them that the fortress was equipped with internal generators, rendering such a plan futile. However, this seemingly futile conversation unexpectedly triggered a dormant memory within Ropo's mind.

Recalling the tumultuous events that had unfolded in the past, Ropo vividly remembered how his son, Sarki, had entrusted him with a key to a safety deposit box, securely nestled within a prominent bank in Lagos, just before his daring escape from prison. Astonishingly, Ropo had never retrieved the contents of this enigmatic box, but now, at this critical juncture of his quest for justice, he couldn't help but wonder if the time had finally arrived to unlock its secrets. With a renewed sense of purpose, Ropo made up his mind to journey back to Lagos and retrieve the key to the safety deposit box. He knew that within its confines lay the potential for a way to get into the palace compound. The thought of what he might discover filled him with a mix of anticipation and trepidation, but he was willing to take the risk. As Ropo boarded the plane to Lagos, he couldn't shake off the feeling that he was on the brink of a breakthrough. The city's bustling streets and familiar sights welcomed him back like an old friend. With each step closer to the bank, Ropo's determination grew stronger, fueled by the hope that the contents of the safety deposit box would finally unveil the solution he had been seeking for so long to completely destroy the Dala Dynasty.

When It Rains It Pours

It was a gloomy and overcast day at the Lake Livingston compound, where Queen Zara and the Algabatas had recently settled into their new residence. However, despite the change in scenery, the atmosphere within the dynasty remained tense and unsettled. On this particular day, a heated argument erupted between Zara and Vincent, a situation that was highly unusual for both individuals. Zara, fueled by her desire to reclaim her throne in the Dala Dynasty, expressed her determination to return to the battlefield. In stark contrast, Vincent vehemently opposed her decision, citing the exorbitant bounty of 5 million dollars placed on her head. He adamantly believed that it would be unwise for her to put herself in harm's way. Zara, confident in her abilities to handle any situation, sought support from E., hoping that he would align with her perspective. However, to her dismay, E. sided with Vincent, sharing his concerns for her safety. He emphasized the importance of keeping her alive, as their future together hinged on it. Frustrated and filled with anger, Zara's wrath was unleashed upon everyone present that day, leaving an indelible mark on the compound. Despite the tension and discord within the dynasty, Queen Zara couldn't shake off the burning desire to reclaim her throne. The weight of her responsibility as a leader weighed heavily on her, and she couldn't ignore the call to fight for her people. Reluctantly, she decided to take Vincent's advice and remain in the United States, but there was an even bigger hurdle to jump.

She decided to take a walk to clear her head. Her mind was consumed by this weighty concern that seemed to grow heavier with each passing step - her precarious immigration status. Having entered the country without a visa, she found herself worried about being discovered and deported. The thought of having to return to her home country sooner than expected added another layer of complexity to her already tumultuous situation.

To address this pressing issue, Ezra Sr., Zara's soon-to-be father-in-law had taken it upon himself to arrange a meeting with an immigration lawyer that very afternoon. Hopeful, the queen stepped back into the chaos, her mind fortified by the brief escape.

However, as if the weight of her immigration concerns weren't enough, the sudden disappearance of the U.S. ambassador, who had played a crucial role in the treaty between the Dala Dynasty and the United States, added an air of mystery and uncertainty to the proceedings. The ambassador's absence seemed to cast a shadow over Zara's already uncertain future, leaving her to wonder if there was any connection between her own predicament and the ambassador's sudden vanishing act.

As she walked, Zara couldn't shake off the unease that settled deep within her. The uncertainty surrounding her immigration status seemed to hang over her like a dark cloud, making her feel even more torn between her love for her home country and her desire for a future with E., the person who had captured her heart. The looming possibility of deportation loomed over her like a sword of Damocles, threatening to sever the ties she had formed in this foreign land.

With each step, Zara's mind raced, contemplating the implications of her immigration status and the ambassador's disappearance. Could there be a connection? Was her own fate intertwined with the ambassador's sudden absence? These questions swirled in her mind, adding to the already overwhelming sense of uncertainty that enveloped her.

As she approached the meeting with the immigration lawyer, Zara couldn't help but feel a mix of hope and trepidation. She desperately needed a solution to her immigration woes, a way to secure her future in this country she had come to call a temporary home.

The meeting with the lawyer held the promise of answers, but also the potential for disappointment. Would this legal expert be able to navigate the complex web of immigration laws and regulations to find a solution for her? Only time would tell.

The road ahead was uncertain, but she was determined to fight for her place in this country, to overcome the obstacles that stood in her way. She had no way of knowing how long it would take her to regain her throne, but this was where God had led her for reasons that yet had been disclosed to her. But she trusted Him, no matter how dark things looked on the horizon. With a deep breath, she approached the house, ready to begin the next chapter of her fight for a future.

The Life Changing Conversation

Ezra Sr. was waiting there with the immigration lawyer, Sam Cooke, when she arrived. She greeted him with a smile and both men stood to welcome her. She sat down and the conversation began. She quickly learned that she would need to leave the country immediately because she did not have a visa and her being a leader from a foreign country with no treaty with America further complicated things. He offered his apologies for the bad news. The lawyer asked Ezra how he was connected to the queen. Ezra responded that the queen was betrothed to his son.

The lawyer asked, "Is there a written contract that states that they are betrothed?"

He replied, "Yes."

Sampson queried, "Who witnessed it?"

"I believe that it was signed by Cardinal Francis Arinzeto."

"Yes, it was signed by the Cardinal", Zara stated. Sam asked, "Do you have a copy?"

"I believe so." She pulled up her copy on the computer and showed it to the lawyer.

He smiled. "Well, there is a way for you to stay in the country..."

"There is? How?" Zara asked.

He enthusiastically responded, "Get married! It says here you were going to do it in December anyway, so make it a June wedding."

Zara looked at Ezra Sr. and he chuckled. "Well, Zara, "I think you and my son have a lot to talk about."

"You will need to do it soon", stated the lawyer. "Legally I am supposed to report you to immigration, but if you get married by Monday, I won't have to do that."

"Monday?" Zara asked.

"Yes, Monday", the lawyer emphasized. "Make sure I'm invited to the wedding as a witness in case there are any complications with immigration, I can vouch for you two."

Zara's heart raced with a mix of excitement and nervousness. The idea of getting married so suddenly seemed daunting, but she couldn't deny the relief that washed over her. She turned to Ezra Sr. and nodded, a grateful smile spreading across her face. "Thank you, so much. We will make sure everything is in order for the wedding on Monday. Do you think E. will agree?"

Ezra Sr. nodded approvingly.

"I 'm glad to hear that", Zara responded.

Ezra Sr. grasped her hand saying, "We'll make sure to handle all the necessary arrangements. Don't worry, everything will be taken care of."

Zara experienced a rush of thankfulness towards Ezra Sr. and couldn't resist sensing a flicker of optimism for her future with his son. While they carried on discussing the arrangements for the wedding, she found herself becoming increasingly thrilled, only to have her joy abruptly shattered.

The Digital Siege

Vincent was livid. Just as they were finally making some headway in opposing the revolutionaries, their entire computer system went down. After a thorough investigation, it was evident that somehow a malicious software virus designed to block access to a computer system had completely caused the mainframe of the dynasty to become inoperable. The Dala Dynasty was currently experiencing a ransomware attack. The attackers had a very specific demand: they wanted the person responsible for the death of Ropo Acheampong's son, Sarki. If the responsible party was not delivered within seven days, the decryption key would forever be lost to the dynasty. With the queen in exile, the country's Council of Elders were racing against time to find a solution. The fate of the decryption key was at the least, uncertain, and failure to meet the attackers' demand could have severe consequences for the entire nation. The Council of Elders had called an emergency task force meeting to address the ransomware attack, and cybersecurity experts from around the world have offered their help. The nation is anxiously awaiting a swift resolution to this crisis. Vincent was in constant contact with them via telephone. It was now obvious; someone was going to have to go back to the dynasty to ensure that the queen regained her throne. He was the most likely candidate. Not only would he have to tell the queen about the ransomware attack, but also that he was leaving. She would be devastated.

Just as he rose from his desk to go to her, she burst into his office with E. trailing behind her. The only bright light in this entire situation was that the young man had risen to the occasion as a suitable suitor. He truly loved the young queen and God knew she needed someone to love her. Vincent had seen him fight fearlessly next to her in the Battle of Shike Hill. She pretended that she didn't notice that he was her constant shadow, but she was taking notes, enough to forgive him for his American arrogance and open her heart again to the possibility of true love.

"Vincent, we are getting married and I would love for you to walk me down the aisle", the queen stated.

"When?" he responded. "Saturday", she said. "So soon, my queen?"

"Yes. Otherwise, I am here illegally".

"I see. Well, congratulations. Perhaps it's best this way"

"Vincent, aren't you happy for us?"

"Yes, Your Highness, but regretfully I have some unfortunate news to share with you".

Zara's hand fell out of E.'s. "What is it now Vincent?"

"Our entire computer system has been attacked by ransomware. We are currently looking for an expert to help us come up with a viable solution, but that will take time, and we don't have much of it", he replied.

"What is it that they want in return?"

"I would prefer not to discuss that right now, your Royal Highness".

"How much money do they want Vincent? she asked.

"Don't you have a wedding to prepare for? It's only two days away. Focus on that mi kekere binrin", he said touching the hand that E. was previously holding.

"While you are preparing for your wedding, the Chancellor and I will handle this minor crisis. Oye?"

Zara continued to quiz the man who was more of a father to her than her own, "Are you sure it doesn't require my attention? It is a national crisis…"

"Your Highness, am I not the head of Security for the Dala Dynasty?"

"Yes, you are…"

"No disrespect… but wasn't I doing this job while you were in diapers", he responded.

Zara stepped back for a moment to contemplate her answer and the room was eerily silent. Everyone in the office knew that her response was critical to Vincent's future.

"This has been a trying time for us all. I will take your advice Vincent because you have never led me down the wrong path but know that you bear full responsibility for the outcome of this malicious act of treason. Oye?"

"Yes, my queen, I do understand. Thank you for giving me the grace to proceed. Please know that I do so with your and our country's future in mind".

"Ko Tope", she replied.

The rest of Zara's day was spent helping the Algabatas plan Saturday's wedding ceremony. Only immediate family were invited to attend, even E.'s younger brothers and sister were excluded from the list for security reasons.

Julia, E.'s mother was ecstatic when she heard the news. When Ezra Sr. tried to discourage her from coming, she temporarily forgot her religion and called him every name but a child of God punctuating the conversation with the following, "Not you or nobody in Africa can stop me from seeing my oldest son get married". If Julia was coming, so was her husband, Curtis.

He wasn't going to be too far behind her and they both would be packing a pistol. After all, this was Texas.

E. had returned to work at his father's construction company as a general manager several days after Ezra Sr. gave him the keys to the house they all were living in.

He spent the better part of the two days before the wedding preparing his men for his two-week absence.

He and Zara could not go on a honeymoon, but the Algabatas were preparing the west wing of the house for the newlywed's glorious staycation as a wedding gift.

The night before the wedding, Ezra Sr., Vincent, and the Algabatas prepared a traditional African meal and celebrated the young couple's upcoming nuptials.

It was a joyous occasion with dancing, an occasional ribbing highlighting the young couple's courtship, and a blessing by Ezra Sr.

As the evening was drawing to an end, while everyone else was comfortable in their beds, Zara decided to catch up on the many messages that were ignored because of the wedding preparation.

She returned to her office and started the process. As she was strolling through them, she ran across an encrypted message that was top secret.

She accessed it and it contained the following message:

Ropo Acheampong refused the monetary offer and is still demanding that we fulfill his original demand for the head of the person who killed his son. The good news is that we have located a company that is very confident that they can decrypt the ransomware called Darktrace Rescue. They assured us that they would beat the attacker's deadline. Please send the $1 Million as previously requested. Respectfully, The Council Of Elders

Queen Zara fell out of her office chair to the floor wailing and crying uncontrollably. Nafisa was the first to respond. Falling on her knees beside the queen, she inquired, "My queen, my queen, what is the matter? Are you ill? Do we need to take you to the hospital?"

Ignoring her, she looks up towards heaven and shouts, "My God, my God, when will it stop? Will every good thing you give to me be ripped from my hands?" E. rushed into the room to find his fiancée crouched down on her knees crying and wailing like someone had died. He picked her up to console her and she pushed away from him. "What's wrong Zara? Whatever it is we can fix it. It's going to be okay, what's wrong? Please Babe tell me what's going on? She looks at him with pure terror in her eyes, "They want to kill you".

CHAPTER 4

The sun rose, casting a golden glow over the exiled queen's chamber. As the rays of light danced on her ebony skin, Queen Zara's heart was heavy with worry. The events of the previous day still haunted her thoughts, for her beloved fiancé, E. Only a handful of people knew who killed Sarki, but the threat of death was too close to home. She had only recently lost her father, and her kingdom and now she could lose the love of her life.

As Queen Zara gazed out of her window, a soft breeze caressed her face, carrying the scent of blooming jasmine. The morning air was filled with a sense of uncertainty as if the world itself was holding its breath. She had always known that her position as queen could endanger those she loved, but she had never imagined that her love for E. would imperil his life not once, but twice.

Her mind drifted back to the day they first met. It was at a grand ball in the royal palace, he was a kind stranger who rescued her from an embarrassing situation. He was her betrothed and she had no clue until the night of the actual wedding announcement.

From the moment that she allowed her heart to be reconciled to the fact that her father, the king, had chosen this man as her husband, their love had blossomed like the wildflowers that painted the African landscape. Their connection had seemed unbreakable, a union forged by destiny. But now, as the threat of revolution loomed over their kingdom, Queen Zara couldn't help but question the consequences of their love.

She knew that marrying E. would further complicate matters. The revolutionaries sought to dismantle the monarchy, and by becoming his wife, she would be tying him to the very institution they despised. Would their love become a liability, endangering not only their lives but also the stability of the kingdom? The weight of responsibility bore down on her, threatening to crush her spirit.

As Queen Zara contemplated her choices, a knock on the bedroom door interrupted her thoughts. Vincent's wrinkled forehead bore the weight of countless years of wisdom, and his eyes sparkled with determination.

"Your Royal Highness," Vincent began, his voice filled with conviction, "I know your heart is heavy with doubt, but love is a force that cannot be denied. E. loves you as fiercely as you love him. Together, you can face any challenge that comes your way."

Queen Zara listened intently, her doubts slowly melting away. She realized that love was not a weakness but a source of strength. It was the glue that held them together in the face of adversity. She knew that the road ahead would be fraught with danger, but she also knew that she couldn't let fear dictate her choices.

With newfound determination, Queen Zara arose from her bed of sorrow determined to make this a great day for the man she loved.

The anxious groom woke up on his wedding day with a mixture of excitement and nerves. As he got ready, he couldn't help but feel a knot in his stomach. E.'s mind raced with thoughts of what could go wrong, and he worried about Zara's changing her mind.

As the hours ticked by, the groom's anxiety only grew. He fidgeted with his tie, unable to find comfort in even the smallest tasks. The weight of the day's expectations loomed over him, and he questioned whether he was truly ready for the commitment he was about to make.

The presence of his father did little to ease his anxiety. He offered kind words and jokes, but he couldn't shake the feeling that he was alone in his fear.

He longed for a moment of solitude to gather his thoughts and calm his racing heart.

When the time finally came to walk down the aisle, the groom's anxiety reached its peak. Doubts flooded his mind, and he wondered if he was truly deserving of his potential partner's love.

But as the groom stood at the altar, waiting for his bride to appear, he took a deep breath and reminded himself of the reasons why he fell in love in the first place. He thought about the moments they shared, the laughter, the support, and the unconditional love they had for each other.

As the Zara entered the room, all of E.'s anxiety melted away. The sight of her radiant smile and the love in her eyes reassured him that this was where he was meant to be. At that moment, he realized that his fears were just a product of his love and the magnitude of the commitment they were about to make.

With renewed confidence, E. exchanged vows with his bride, promising to love and cherish her for the rest of their lives. As they sealed their vows with a kiss, the groom's anxiety was replaced with a sense of peace and joy. He knew that no matter what challenges they faced, they would face them together.

The anxious groom had transformed into a confident husband, ready to embark on a new chapter of his life. As the wedding celebration began, he let go of his worries and enjoyed the day with his loved ones. He knew that the love and support surrounding him would carry him through any anxieties he might face in the future.

In the end, the anxious groom realized that his fears were just a natural part of the wedding day jitters. The love he shared with Zara was stronger than any anxiety or doubt. As they danced their first dance as husband and wife, he couldn't help but feel a deep sense of gratitude for the woman who had chosen to spend her life with him.

A Honeymoon on the Gentle Waves

As the morning sun cast its golden rays across the vast expanse of Lake Victoria, a small yacht glided gracefully through the calm waters. On the deck stood Queen Zara, and her newlywed husband, Prince Ezra. This was their first adventure as husband and wife, a brief honeymoon getaway before the weight of their royal duties settled upon their shoulders once again.

The gentle breeze kissed their faces, carrying the scent of wildflowers and the promise of freedom. Queen Zara's ebony skin glowed in the sunlight, her vibrant traditional attire a striking contrast against the azure backdrop of the lake. With a radiant smile, she took Ezra's hand, their fingers intertwining like a bridge between their two worlds.

As the yacht sailed on, the calm waters of Lake Victoria gradually gave way to a narrow passage leading to the Gulf of Mexico. The landscape transformed, with lush greenery giving way to mangroves and the distant sound of crashing waves. The air grew salty and invigorating, filling their lungs with a sense of adventure.

For Queen Zara, this journey represented more than just a honeymoon. It was a chance to explore a world beyond the borders of the Dala Dynasty, to step into new territories, and discover the beauty and diversity that lay beyond her kingdom's shores. And as they sailed further away from their lakeside home, she felt her spirit soar, liberated from the constraints of her crown and responsibilities.

As the yacht glided along, Queen Zara and Prince Ezra found solace in each other's company. They laughed, they dreamed, and they shared secrets only lovers could know. Their conversations echoed the promise of a future filled with love, adventure, and the shared goal of bringing prosperity to her people once again.

But amidst the joy and tranquility, a sense of anticipation lingered in the air. Queen Zara's heart swelled with both excitement and trepidation as the yacht ventured further into uncharted waters.

Will this idyllic honeymoon be everything they hoped for, or will unforeseen obstacles threaten their newfound happiness? Only time would tell. But for now, as the yacht sailed towards the horizon, Queen Zara and Prince Ezra stood tall, ready to face whatever lay ahead, hand in hand, their love a beacon guiding them through the unknown.

As the sun began to set, casting a warm golden glow over the horizon, Queen Zara and Prince Ezra found themselves lost in a sea of possibilities, unscathed by the past and wrapped in the arms of what could be. It was at this very moment that Queen Zara felt an assurance that she would regain her crown, and this time she would have the man she loved by her side. With each passing moment, their love grew stronger, anchoring them to the present and giving them the strength to navigate whatever challenges awaited them. And so, hand in hand, they embraced the uncertainty, knowing that together they could conquer anything that came their way. At least that is what she thought in the glow of her marital bliss, but reality would soon unveil the true measure of their unconventional union.

Back to Reality

The honeymoon was heavenly, but all good things eventually have to end. It was as if she had stepped from one dimension to another when the boat docked at her resort hideaway. Every member of her security team stood at attention like toy soldiers lined up for a military inspection in anticipation of the young couple's arrival. They were barely at the house when she was given a Top-Secret envelope updating her on the revolution in her country. There were moments when she tried to escape back into the blissful memories of that glorious week, but they escaped her. The weight of ruling from afar was stealing everything she had left inside her inner being to fight this battle. How could she be losing after God had assured her she would win?

The honeymoon had come to an end, and Queen Zara found herself wrestling with a dark forbidding that heavily plagued her. When she wasn't putting out fires or alone at night in the quiet of her bedroom listening to E.'s quiet breathing, it mercilessly taunted her. The loss of her kingdom and the challenges of being a new wife weighed heavily on her shoulders. Feeling overwhelmed, she turned to God in prayer, seeking guidance and assistance.

One of the main sources of support and counsel in her life, Vincent, her trusted advisor, had returned to The Dala Dynasty to lead the military forces working on restoring her to the throne. His absence only added to her feelings of loneliness and despair.

As Queen Zara poured her heart out to God, she sought solace and strength to face the difficulties that lay ahead. She prayed for the restoration of her kingdom, for wisdom to navigate her role as a wife, and for the return of her trusted advisor.

In her moments of vulnerability, Queen Zara found comfort in her faith. She reminded herself that she was not alone, that God was with her, listening to her prayers and guiding her steps. She drew strength from the belief that there was a purpose to her struggles and that she would emerge stronger on the other side, but she needed help… spiritual help. One day, she discovered this…

"Be anxious for nothing, but in everything by prayer and supplication, with thanksgiving, let your requests be made known to God; and the peace of God, which surpasses all understanding, will guard your hearts and minds through Christ Jesus"

(PHILIPPIANS 6-7, NKJV).

She recognized that at the root of her depression was the anxiousness she was feeling about regaining her kingdom. Yet, she had so many other things to be grateful for: her husband's love, the loyalty of the Algabatas, her wonderful father-in-love, the beautiful home she lived in, the list was endless.

Zara decided to thank God for what He had done for her and to ask Him for what she felt she needed, and that was someone to help her better understand her current role as a leader, a wife, and a Christian.

As Queen Zara poured her heart out to God, she sought solace and strength to face the difficulties that lay ahead. She prayed for the restoration of her kingdom, for wisdom to navigate her role as a wife, and for the return of her trusted advisor.

The Unexpected Mentor

One day while the queen was upstairs in her prayer closet, there was a knock on the front door. It was an unusual occurrence because they rarely had visitors, and this one was unexpected and unannounced. Nafisa cautiously answered the door. Standing there in the bright morning sunshine was a middle-aged Caucasian woman who reminded her of Reba McIntyre, about 5 ft 2 in, with sharp observant blue eyes, blazing red hair, a Texas twang, genteel, and confident.

Nafisa greeted her with a, "May I help you?"

The woman responded, "My name is Patricia Emerson, and God sent me".

Nafisa, baffled by her response, was even more so to hear the voice of the queen behind her.

"Let her in. God told me that she was coming".

Nafisa stepped aside and allowed Patricia Emerson to enter the mansion. As they made their way to the living room, Patricia explained that she had been led to Queen Zara through a series of divine signs and visions. Zara instructed Leilah to bring some refreshments for their guest, and she encouraged Patricia to get comfortable. The ladies settled in for a long afternoon of sharing.

Patricia started with her personal testimony with Zara. "God has a unique way of getting us to where he wants us. For the past few weeks, he has been sending me dreams of Africa. My husband and I used to be missionaries in Mozambique and Zimbabwe, and now we run a training center to equip young people like yourself to carry the gospel around the world. He moved us back home when it was apparent that the United States was becoming a mission field".

Zara sitting spellbound was intrigued, she asked, "How many years were you in Africa?"

Wiggling in her chair, Patricia responded, "Wait a minute Queen Zara, I need to get out of this jacket". She took it off and put it on the settee beside her. "Now, let's get back to our conversation. We were in Africa for twenty years and I almost lost my beloved Jim to malaria, but God spared him. When he was miraculously healed, we just picked up where we left off and started doing the work of the Lord all over again. But I digress, let me get down to why I'm here and how I got here in the first place".

"Are you comfortable now?" asked Zara.

"Yes, I am, thank you. This Texas heat is not for the weak of heart, I tell you". She replied.

"My husband and I live in a little town on the outside of Houston called Sugar Land. I was driving down the street on my way to the mall and I heard the Lord say, 'You won't be doing any shopping today. I have a special assignment for you'. I was headed to 610, but when the Lord says to go somewhere, you better go or you'll end up like Jonah", she chuckled.

Zara responded, "The man who was swallowed by a big fish… am I correct?"

"Absolutely", said Patricia. "I see that you have been reading your Bible, that's good, real good". She reached down to smooth a protruding wrinkle out of her skirt. "I 'm afraid I 've put on a few pounds since returning to the States".

"The food is considerably different here. It's good but fattening. But that's not my only excuse. I've acquired the 'honeymoon 20'. I was recently married", Zara proudly exclaims.

"So are you saying that you put on twenty extra pounds from good loving and good eating?" replied Patricia.

The blushing queen replied, "I 'm afraid so", and they both laughed.

"Well you look absolutely lovely with your extra 'honeymoon 20,'" Patricia replied. "I'm afraid I can't claim that as my excuse. I just love good food. So back to my reason for being here. I had no idea where I was going. I kept listening to the Holy Spirit and he led me here. I was glad I gassed up before I left. Now Zara, may I call you Zara?"

"Of course. Are you comfortable? Is it too hot in here?' the queen inquires.

"Well, I think I 'm flashin' with all of the excitement… when a woman reaches a certain age things start to change". She leaned toward the queen and whispered, "This girdle is killin' me".

An astonished Zara responded, "Oh my… Leliah please go into my closet and get a mumu for Patricia". Leilah immediately obeys.

"No. No. No. you don't have to do that. I'll be okay…" she protested.

Zara responded, "It's already done. There's a changing room in the first bedroom on the left. Feel free to relieve yourself and when you come back, we will have lunch".

Patricia was led to the bedroom by Leliah, and she returned with an elaborate purple African Ankara mid-knee length dress with a gold wax shawl collar.

"My my, this is absolutely gorgeous", Patricia said.

"It is yours my new friend to keep. Please accept this as a gift of my appreciation for your obedience to God. You are literally an answer to prayer". Zara responded.

Patricia returned to the settee and the women had a casual conversation over a delectable lunch served by Leliah. She spoke with conviction and a sense of purpose, assuring Queen Zara that she was sent to further her discipleship. Intrigued and hopeful, Queen Zara listened intently, sensing that this encounter was a turning point in her journey. Patricia Emerson shared stories of her own experiences, recounting how she had faced adversity and emerged stronger through her unwavering faith. She spoke of the power of divine intervention and the miracles that can occur when one fully surrenders to God's plan.

Zara was like a new sponge anxiously soaking up everything she said. Both women sat beside each other emersed in their conversation. Patricia led Zara to Jeremiah 29:11, reassuring her that God had a good plan for her life regardless of the things she faced, it eventually would work out for God's good. She affirmed that he used the difficult things in our lives to mold us and shape us in his image and prepare us to fulfill our purpose. We have to trust him and trust the process. She assured Zara that God knew her intimately before she was even born. She showed the young queen Jeremiah 1:5 (NKJV), which states: "Before I formed you in the womb I knew you; Before you were born I sanctified you; I ordained you a prophet to the nations", as proof.

Patricia praised her for acknowledging the significance of prayer. She emphasized that it served as our means of connecting with God. She proceeded to educate the queen as if they

had been in a mentor-mentee relationship for an extended period of time.

"Zara, there is an acronym that I use when I am teaching our young missionaries about prayer. It is A.C.T. The A is a reminder to first ACKNOWLEDGE God through praise. The C is a reminder to CONFESS our sins and weaknesses to God, and the T is a reminder to THANK God for his mercy and grace. If you want a great example of this, go to The Lord's Prayer in Matthew 6. Jesus taught us so much about how to live a victorious Christian life". She lifts her bible, "We just have to read the instruction manual!"

Patricia received a notification on her cellphone and she excused herself from the room. When she returned, she apologetically said that she had to leave because her husband's flight had been delayed and she had to teach this evening at the Center in his absence. But she assured Zara that she would be back to finish their conversation. The two women set an appointment for the next day around the same time. Before she left, she prayed a powerful prayer over E. and Zara's home, their marriage, and Zara's continued growth in the Lord. They embraced each other like long-lost friends and bid their goodbyes with the anticipation of God doing a complete work in each of them during their time together.

Queen Zara felt a renewed sense of hope and determination, realizing that Patricia's arrival was not a mere coincidence, but a sign that her prayers were being answered. With Patricia by her side, Queen Zara was ready to embark on a new chapter, trusting in God's guidance every step of the way. She couldn't wait to share her new adventure and friend with E. when he got home from work.

Zara decided to take a well-deserved nap before her beloved came home and just as she was about to drift off there was a ruckus outside her window. She reluctantly relinquished her pillow and went to the balcony to see what was going on. To her merriment, Leilah was holding a boy by the collar of his shirt in the air. He was kicking and screaming trying to escape her clutches, but being the woman warrior she was, she had the situation under control.

"What's happening down there?" she inquired.

"I caught this little one down at the lake, Your Majesty", she replied. On the ground laid a discarded fishing pole and a tackle box that had seen better years.

The boy looked up and was instantly mesmerized. He'd never seen a woman that possessed such exotic beauty. Her braided hair gently blowing in the wind, skin as smooth as cocoa butter, and a voice that seemed to sing in his ears. Surely she was from heaven.

The queen assessed the situation and decided to further investigate the matter. "I 'll be down in a minute". She grabbed her robe and hurried to the deck. Upon her arrival, she scrutinized him from head to toe. His tattered tennis shoes, wrinkled shirt, and knee-high pants spoke of poverty. He was in desperate need of a haircut and a bath.

"Put him down", she commanded. He shuddered. "What's your name?" He raised his head to look at her and mumbled, "Princeton".

"Well Princeton, can you tell me what prompted you to visit us today?" she asked.

"I was just fishing. I was here way before you arrived. No one was living here… and I didn't think it would hurt anyone if I caught a few fish. I never came near the house", he responded.

"I see. So do you come every day?" she asked.

"No ma'am, just when my mom doesn't have anything for dinner", he said shuffling his feet.

Zara's heart broke. She turned to Leliah saying, "Go get some muffins and milk for our esteemed guest. She turns to their young captive saying, Princeton, would you like to join me for some snacks?"

His stomach grumbled in response. He shook his head in agreement. The two of them sat on the deck for another hour talking. The queen strategically found out that the boy and his mom lived in a nearby hotel. She worked during the day, so he was left to cultivate his own adventures. He found the pier one day when he was exploring and decided to try to learn how to fish. A stranger at the hotel gave him the rod and tackle box after he washed his car. He apologized for sneaking on the property to fish, but when he brought it home, his mother was overjoyed. He liked making her happy, and she hadn't been for a long time. Especially after his father died.

At that moment, Queen Zara decided that she would do everything in her power to help her industrious captive. She instructed Leliah to take him home by way of the grocery store and she permitted him to come fish anytime he wanted to. She also handed him an envelope and instructed him not to open it, but to give it to his mother when she arrived home from work. He assured her he would but asked meekly if it was a note about his trespassing. She emphatically shook her head "no." She responded, "You were an honored guest in our home today, not a trespasser".

When his mom opened the envelope later that evening, she fell on the bed in astonishment amid ten crisp thousand-dollar bills.

CHAPTER 5

*T*rue to her word, Patricia returned the next day, wearing another designer suit and tight girdle. Leilah was instructed to go get another muumuu from Zara's closet. The two women agreed after much debate that payment for Patricia's instruction would be done in African muumuus until they completed Zara's training.

The topic of the day was the promises of God. Patricia explained that she had extensive knowledge of scripture and a deep understanding of God's promises because she had served the lord for over 50 years. She believed that God's promises were not just words written in the Bible, but living and active truths that could transform lives. She shared that there were over

5000 promises of God in the bible. She encouraged the young queen to put her focus on God's promises instead of her troubles.

She also shared the importance of understanding who God is and introduced Zara to the names of God which reinforced the promises he made to all believers. Some of the examples she used were El Roi - The God Who Sees, Jehovah Nissi - The Banner, our Covering, and Jehovah Shalom - The God of Peace. Patricia specifically used these illustrations because of the struggles the young women were experiencing. She reiterated the fact that God is omnipresent and sees all. So Zara need not question whether he is with her, because he is always there; at all times. She shared the story of Hagar. As the head of state, Queen Zara needed to be reassured that there was a higher authority over her that had her best interest at heart. Patricia told her that he placed her there because he had a special plan for her as a ruler of the Dala Dynasty. She took her to the Songs of Solomon 2:4 and shared, "He brought me to the banqueting house, And his banner over me *was* love. His intent is to love us, even to the point where he has promised us that nothing can separate us from his love". And finally, she shared with Zara that God's peace is readily available to her as a believer because he is the Prince of Peace.

Patricia also shared examples of biblical figures who had experienced the faithfulness of God's promises, such as Abraham, Moses, and David. She emphasized that these promises were not limited to the past but were available to Queen Zara and all believers today.

Patricia encouraged Queen Zara to hold onto God' s promises during challenging times. She explained that God' s promises provided hope, strength, and direction. They were a source of comfort and assurance that God was with them and working on their behalf.

Patricia reminded Queen Zara of promises such as God' s faithfulness, provision, protection, and guidance. She urged her to trust in these promises and to rely on God's word as the ultimate source of truth and wisdom.

To help Queen Zara navigate her role as a wife, Patricia shared promises related to marriage and relationships. She spoke about the importance of love, forgiveness, and unity in a marriage, referring to verses such as Ephesians 5:22-33 and 1 Peter 3:1-7.

Patricia also highlighted promises of God' s blessing on the family and the importance of raising children in the fear and knowledge of the Lord.

In addition to marriage, Patricia discussed promises related to the restoration of her kingdom. She reminded Queen Zara of God' s promise to bring justice and righteousness and to establish His kingdom on earth.

Patricia encouraged Queen Zara to pray and believe for the restoration of her kingdom, trusting that God would fulfill His promises in His perfect timing.

Throughout their conversation, Patricia emphasized the importance of faith and obedience in experiencing the fulfillment of God' s promises. She encouraged Queen Zara to remain steadfast in her faith, to seek God' s will in all things, and to align her actions with His word. Patricia assured Queen Zara that as she walked in faith and obedience, she would witness the manifestation of God' s promises in her life and in the Dala Dynasty.

By the end of their mentorship session, Queen Zara felt inspired and empowered. She had a newfound understanding of God's promises and their relevance to her life. Patricia's teachings ignited a burning desire within Queen Zara to deepen her relationship with God and to fully embrace His promises. With Patricia's guidance, Queen Zara was determined to live a life grounded in faith, trusting in God's promises, and leading her kingdom with wisdom and righteousness. As Queen Zara embarked on her journey of faith and leadership, she knew that challenges would arise. However, she was now equipped with the knowledge of God' s promises and the assurance that He would be with her every step of the way. With Patricia' s guidance, Queen Zara was ready to face any obstacle, knowing that God' s faithfulness, provision, protection, and guidance would never waver. She was determined to lead her kingdom with love, forgiveness, and unity, trusting in the promises of God' s blessing on her family and the restoration of her kingdom.

E. and Zara's Date Night

Queen Zara pleasantly surprised Prince E. with an impromptu date night at their lavish pool. As he returned home and was greeted by Queen Zara wearing a sexy black dress with a plunging neckline, and a thigh-high slit, revealing just the right amount of skin to leave him captivated. It clung to her curves, accentuating her figure, she was a picture-perfect epitome of elegance and sophistication. The pool house was adorned with flickering candles, his favorite dishes served, and romantic melodies filling the air. Zara got the idea after reading the Songs of Solomon 6:3 which states, "I am my beloved's and my beloved is mine".

E. was taken aback by the thoughtful gesture and was filled with gratitude for Queen Zara's love and effort. They spent the evening enjoying each other's company, basking in the ambiance of the poolside setting. This intimate and romantic date night strengthened their bond and reminded them of the deep love they share.

The evening culminated with a late-night swim. As they floated in the pool, gazing at the starry night sky, Queen Zara expressed her gratitude for Prince E.' s unwavering support and love. She reflected on how their relationship has grown stronger over time, and how their shared faith has been the foundation of their love. In this moment of tranquility, they both felt a renewed sense of purpose and commitment to each other, knowing that together they can overcome any challenge that comes their way.

As the night comes to a close, Queen Zara and Prince E. exchange heartfelt vows of love and commitment. They promise to continue nurturing their relationship, prioritizing communication, and always seeking God' s guidance in their journey together. With their hearts full of love and their spirits uplifted, Queen Zara and E. retired for the night, knowing that their bond would only grow stronger with each passing day.

The Morning After

Zara and E. were awakened by the mesmerizing sound of birds singing a melodic love song. The queen was the heavy sleeper in the duo, it was very unusual for her to leave the comfort of their bed before him. But today, they'd awakened simultaneously to each of their surprise. Queen Zara woke up feeling a sense of contentment and happiness. She opened her eyes to find E. lying next to her, his gaze filled with adoration. They exchanged a soft smile, their hearts still connected from the intimate moments they shared the night before.

As the morning light filtered through the curtains, Queen Zara's hand gently caressed E.'s cheek, tracing the contours of his face. Her touch was feather-light, sending shivers down his spine. She leaned in closer, her lips brushing against his, teasingly. Their breaths mingle, creating an intoxicating mix of warmth and desire.

At that moment, time seemed to stand still as their lips met in a passionate and sensual kiss. Their mouths moved in perfect harmony; their tongues danced with a fiery intensity. The taste of each other lingered on their lips, a sweet and addictive flavor that awakened their senses.

Their bodies pressed against each other, the heat between them intensified with every passing second. Queen Zara's fingers entangled in Prince E.'s hair, pulling him closer as she deepened the kiss. Prince E.'s hands explored the curves of Queen Zara's body, tracing the outline of her silhouette, igniting a fire within them both.

Their kiss was a symphony of desire, a testament to their love and longing for each other. It spoke volumes without the need for words, conveying their deepest emotions and desires. In this moment, they were lost in each other, consumed by the passion that burns… the telephone rings. E. groans and reluctantly rolls over to answer it.

"Hello", he mumbles, pulling the object of his desire closer.

"Good morning son, I 've got Sam Cooke on the line. He has some good news for Zara. Is she there?" asks Ezra Sr.

"Where else is she going to be Pops? We're newlyweds… remember you told us you wanted lots of grandchildren". E. responds jokingly.

"Well now… is she blushing?" his father responded.

Zara took the phone from E. with a glare, she put it on speaker, and answered his question, "Totally Dad! Good morning Mr. Cooke, how are you?"

"Fine, Queen Zara, but obviously not as fine as you are…" he replied.

Ignoring his solacious comment she asked, "You have some good news for me?"

"I reached out to an acquaintance of mine who works at the State Department and informed him about your predicament. He found your narrative fascinating and expressed a desire to assist you. As a result, he arranged for you to meet with the President of the United States tomorrow at 2:00 p.m. in Washington D.C. Will you be able to make it?" he asked eagerly.

"Of course", she responds quickly her breath catching in surprise.

"Great," he responded, "You will only have ten minutes. I recommend that you be prepared with a concise petition for his help. You don't want to waste a second of this opportunity".

E. chimed in, "We won't. Thank you, Mr. Cooke".

"My pleasure", he replied. "I have a 9:00 a.m. meeting. I 'll keep my fingers crossed for you two. Goodbye".

"Goodbye." The group replied.

Ezra Sr. spoke next, "I have made arrangements for you to leave today at 4:00 p.m. A car will be there at 3:00 p.m. to pick you up to take you to the airport. You should arrive in Washington D.C. at 7:00 p.m. EST. A driver will be there to take your entourage to the Waldorf Astoria for a two-night stay. I made the reservation for four. Unfortunately, I won't be able to accompany you because of a prior commitment but know I will be praying every second that you are at the White House for God's favor and your success. Son, if you could come by the office, I have a package for you. I also need an update on the Morrison Project before you leave. I know you had an important meeting with his team today".

"Yes, sir", he replied, "I 'll be there in about an hour. Thanks, Pops for making the arrangements and everything".

Ezra Sr. earnestly responds with, "It brings me joy, my son. Zara, my lovely daughter, there is no need to be concerned about security as I have made the necessary arrangements. The Divine is granting you opportunities that cannot be hindered by any human force. You have been predestined for this very moment. Never forget your true identity - you are a beloved offspring of the Almighty and the rightful heir of the Dala Dynasty. I have unwavering faith in you, so place your crown upon your head once again and enter the president' s office with grace and confidence. My love for you knows no bounds and will forever be a constant reliable force every second that I live and breathe on the earth."

Tears filling her eyes and joy filling her heart, Zara responded, "I love you too Dad. How can I ever repay you for your kindness?"

"It' s not required. We' re family! Simply continue to bring joy to my son' s life and give me grandchildren, and I'll be content. Goodbye". Ezra Sr. ended the call with a heart full of gratitude. His son had come far since his days on *The Missionary Maiden*. On bended knees, he began to express his gratitude to God for all the blessings bestowed upon him and his loved ones, and God smiles.

A Midday Mentoring Session

As the morning sun cast long shadows across the deck, Zara couldn't' t shake the sense of urgency that gripped her. She sat on the living room sofa staring out the window, debating how to break the news.

With a sigh, she squared her shoulders and decided that transparency was the best option. There was a knock on the door and Leliah opened it and greeted Patrica with kind words.

Zara rose to her feet saying, "Right on time." she greeted her with a warm smile. "Patricia, there' s something I need to discuss with you," her voice carrying a note of seriousness. As she explained the unexpected summons to Washington D.C. for a crucial meeting, she watched her mentor's expression shift from curiosity to understanding. The gravity of the situation hung in the air.

"I understand. Duty calls," Patricia said, her gaze meeting hers with a mixture of pride and concern. "We can always reschedule our meeting. Your commitment to your responsibilities is commendable."

Relief washed over Zara as she realized her mentor's support remained steadfast. They managed to discuss some key points, albeit briefly, before she had to leave. That day's discussion was on how the enemy uses distractions to pull your focus off of God. Patricia used the example of Eve and Satan. Eve knew what God said about eating the forbidden fruit, but she let the opinion of someone else influence her obedience.

He manipulated her understanding of what was said by reiterating that nothing could be that bad (surely you won't die if you do eat it).

Eve took the bait and stepped out of the realm of God's protection and was exposed to a different world, one full of evil, condemnation, and shame. (Genesis 3:2-4) She encouraged Zara to know who her enemies are and to act accordingly. When in doubt, ask God and he will show you what that person's true intentions are. The two women ended their session in prayer.

Patricia specifically asked that God's favor would surround Zara and E. like an impenetrable shield.

The meeting may have been cut short, but the bond between mentor and mentee only grew stronger in the face of unexpected challenges.

As Zara boarded the plane to Washington D.C., she couldn't' t help but feel grateful for the guidance that had prepared her for such pivotal moments in her journey.

Hello Mr. President

Queen Zara, accompanied by her husband, made a grand entrance as they arrived at the iconic White House, the official residence of the President of the United States. Their purpose for this visit was to engage in a crucial discussion with the President, seeking his assistance in reclaiming her rightful crown. This meeting held immense significance for the queen, as it represented a pivotal moment in her quest to regain her power and authority. The White House, with its historical significance and political influence, served as the backdrop for this important rendezvous, adding an air of gravitas to the proceedings. As the queen and her husband stepped foot into the White House, they were greeted with the utmost respect and courtesy, befitting their royal status. The anticipation and tension in the air were palpable, as both parties understood the weight of the matter at hand. The queen, adorned in regal attire, exuded confidence, and determination, ready to present her case to the President. Her husband, a steadfast pillar of support, stood by her side, offering unwavering encouragement and solidarity. The corridors of power resonated with the echoes of their footsteps, as they made their way toward the President' s office, where the crucial conversation would take place. The queen' s heartbeat with a mix of hope and apprehension, knowing that the outcome of this meeting could shape the course of her future.

The President, fully aware of the queen's predicament, had graciously agreed to meet with her, recognizing the importance of maintaining strong diplomatic relations. The grandeur of the White House served as a symbol of the United States' commitment to international cooperation and support. Inside the walls of this historic building, the queen and her husband found themselves at the epicenter of power and influence, surrounded by the rich tapestry of American history. The meeting room, adorned with exquisite furnishings and stately portraits of past leaders, sets the stage for this momentous encounter. The queen's eyes were drawn to the portraits, each representing a chapter in the nation's story, reminding her of the resilience and determination required to overcome challenges.

As they entered the President's office, the queen's gaze was met by the resolute figure of President Roberto Salazar, who stood tall behind the desk, ready to engage in a discussion that could shape the destiny of a nation. The atmosphere was charged with a sense of purpose and urgency, as the queen and her husband took their seats, ready to present their case. The President, known for his diplomatic prowess and strategic thinking, listened attentively, fully aware of the weight of responsibility that rests upon his shoulders. The queen's words flowed with eloquence and conviction, as she articulated her desire to reclaim her crown and restore stability to her kingdom. Her husband, a trusted confidant, interjected with supporting arguments, emphasizing the importance of international cooperation and the shared values between their two nations. The President, displayed a keen understanding of the complexities involved, asked probing questions, seeking to fully grasp the nuances of the situation. What was initially scheduled as a brief exchange turned into a two-hour meeting. The conversation is extremely robust with each party presenting their perspectives and exploring potential avenues for collaboration.

"Imagine a scenario where the United States lacked a commander-in-chief, Mr. President. Unfortunately, my country has been enduring a lack of genuine leadership for more than three months now. The loss of my father has added to the devastation experienced by my people. Throughout my entire life, I have been prepared to become an honorable and principled leader. It deeply saddens me that due to the ongoing civil war, I am unable to be present for my people whom I hold an unwavering love for", states Queen Zara.

The president acknowledged her dilemma and said, "I deeply sympathize with you and your country. It is impossible to confirm the existence of a past agreement during your father' s lifetime. Regrettably, we are unable to find the American Ambassador for that area who could verify its validity".

Queen Zara's determination was unwavering, her resolve strengthened by the support and encouragement she received from her husband.

E. responded in support of his wife, "The American ambassador was there at our betrothal ceremony. He was one of the witnesses who signed our agreement. I can prove it. Here he is in this video making remarks".

"May I?" asked the president. When his aide got E.'s cellphone, he put it on speaker and handed it to the President.

A loud booming midwestern voice blasted from the telephone:

> *"It is with great pleasure that the United States of America announces its diplomatic alliance with the Dala Dynasty, under the esteemed leadership of Oba Jaiye. We express our utmost gratitude for the honor of witnessing this joyous union between your beautiful daughter and an outstanding American gentleman. We anticipate a fruitful and prosperous relationship between our nations that will endure for generations to come."*

"Ay Dios mío", exclaimed the President. "He does confirm our alliance in this video. Can we have a copy of this?"

"Si", responds E.

"Do you speak Spanish?" The President inquired.

Yes. Both my wife and I speak Spanish fluently. "Cierto mi amor?"

"Sí, mi amor". "Asombroso!"

"Señor presidente es el lenguaje del amor, no?" Queen Zara questioned.

The President nodded his head in affirmation. They continued the rest of their conversation in Spanish to the delight of The President.

Recognizing the queen' s passion and commitment, he acknowledged the significance of her cause and pledged his support in finding a resolution.

The meeting concluded with a sense of optimism and renewed hope, as both parties committed to working together towards a common goal. As the queen and her husband bid farewell to the President and left the White House, they carried with them a renewed sense of purpose and determination.

The journey to reclaim the crown may be challenging, but with the support of the United States, the queen was emboldened to face whatever lied ahead. The White House stands as a testament to the enduring power of collaboration and the pursuit of justice. The queen' s visit to the White House marked a significant chapter in her quest for restoration, a chapter that will be remembered in the annals of history.

CHAPTER 6

The sun hung high in the cloudless sky, casting its scorching rays over the arid plains of North Africa. The once peaceful country, now a battleground, reverberated with the sounds of gunfire and explosions. The air was thick with the acrid scent of smoke and the cries of the wounded. In the tumultuous landscape of North Africa, the fierce civil war raged on within the geographical boundaries of the Dala Dynasty. The revolutionists, driven by a passionate desire and greed, had gained significant momentum in their fight against the young queen's army.

Amidst the chaos, a determined group of dissidents, clad in tattered uniforms and carrying rifles, advance towards a fortified government compound in the northern part of the dynasty. Their faces etched with determination and malicious intent, they moved forward, their footsteps resonated with a newfound confidence.

As they approached the compound, the rebels unleashed a barrage of gunfire, seeking to suppress the enemy' s defenses. The deafening noise of their weapons echoed through the dusty streets, drowning out the sound of happiness and contentment that has lingered for years.

Suddenly, an explosion erupted from within the compound. The revolutionists' meticulous planning had paid off, as they breached the outer walls with precision. The regime' s soldiers were caught off guard and overwhelmed by the revolutionists' determination, scrambling to defend their positions.

The rebels pushed forward; their ranks grew with each passing moment as more fighters joined the fray. They employed guerrilla tactics, utilizing the maze-like streets and buildings to their advantage. They moved swiftly, taking cover behind crumbling structures and strategically picking off their enemies. The second most impenetrable compound in the dynasty was now a battlefield, with revolutionists and regime soldiers engaged in a fierce and chaotic struggle.

Amidst the chaos, Ropo Acheampong emerged from the ranks of the dissenters. With a commanding presence and unwavering determination, they rallied their comrades, urging them to fight on.

He shouted: "Tiwa ni isegun. Gbogbo ohun ti a ni lati ṣe ni gbigba". (The victory is ours. All we have to do is take it.)

"Where is your virgin queen? Probably somewhere laid up with her American lover. She has deserted you and left you here to fend for yourselves. When will you get it through your thick skulls that she doesn't care what happens to you? You call her a 'warrior queen'… harrumph, she's nothing but a coward. I sent her running away like a dog with its tail between her legs. You love her… then die for her". Ropo started shooting indiscriminately into the air. "Anyone who renounces her and her throne will get to live today. Otherwise, say goodbye to your family and friends because I am the new commander-in-chief of this dynasty!"

These words resonated through the dusty air, fueling the revolutionists' resolve and inspiring them to push even harder.

As the battle raged on, the revolutionists gained ground, inch by hard-fought inch. The regime' s soldiers, now disoriented and demoralized, began to retreat. The revolutionists seized the opportunity, pressing their advantage and driving the enemy forces out of the compound.

Victory was within reach, and the insurgents tasted it. They stood united; their spirits lifted by this significant triumph. With the capture of one of the key strongholds, they had sent a powerful message to their exiled queen - their fight would not be silenced.

The revolutionists, now in control of the compound, began the arduous task of securing the area and tending to the wounded. They had set up makeshift medical stations, providing much-needed care to their comrades. The streets that were once filled with happiness were now filled with despair, as the revolutionists celebrated their hard-won victory and prepared for the challenges that lie ahead.

As the dust settled and the celebration subsided, the rebels turned their attention to the next phase of their mission. They gathered in a makeshift command center, strategizing and planning their next moves. With the compound secured, they now had a base of operations from which to launch further attacks against the new regime. The agitators understood that their fight was far from over, but they were emboldened by their recent victory and ready to continue their unjustified pursuit.

Ropo was a master war strategist at heart. He decided not to limit the fight to the borders of the Dala Dynasty. As the leader of the conflict, he managed to rally neighboring countries to join the fight. How did he achieve this? By enticing these countries with promises of land and a share of the kingdom' s wealth. Such incentives had proven to be effective in garnering support from these neighboring nations before.

It was worth noting that the Dala Dynasty, despite being a relatively small country, held significant importance due to its role as a major supplier of oil to Egypt. This fact added an extra layer of intensity to the ongoing conflict.

The African queen' s army, which was at the forefront of the battle, found itself in a challenging situation. The odds seemed stacked against them, and the outcome appeared bleak.

The civil war in the Dala Dynasty was not just a localized conflict but rather a complex web of alliances and power struggles. The leader' s ability to convince neighboring countries to join the fight showcases his political prowess. By promising land and a share of the kingdom's wealth, he tapped into the desires and ambitions of these nations, effectively solidifying their support.

As the African queen' s army faced the challenges posed by the civil war, they found themselves in a precarious position. The odds were not in their favor, and the outcome seemed uncertain.

The Battle is Not Over

Vincent hadn't had a home cooked meal in ages. In the six weeks he had been back in his homeland he had seen his wife once. He was sick of this war. Recent reports had placed Ropo in the northern part of the dynasty. He'd commandeered one of their most powerful governmental compounds. It hadn't even occurred to him that he had that kind of manpower. While they were experiencing some victories in the south, he was strategically plotting to take down the northern compound.

It looked like Queen Zara was going to have to come back. He'd done everything in his power to avoid that. But things were now at a point where the people, even the Council of Elders, were questioning her loyalty.

Vincent cursed under his breath as he forcefully punched the wall in frustration, leaving behind a bloody mess. The agreement had been clear - Vincent would take care of matters back home while Ezra Sr. provided the financial support for the war effort. Ezra Sr. had fulfilled his part of the deal without fail. He had not.

In moments like these, he couldn't' t help but long for Oba Jaiye' s presence, someone who knew how to ruthlessly deal with enemies. If Oba Jaiye were still alive, Ropo' s head would have been displayed on a pike in the compound square long ago. A dark chuckle escaped from Vincent as he entertained this thought.

Just as he was going to the medicine cabinet to get a bandage for his injured hand, his telephone rang. He attempted to pick it up with his good hand and almost dropped it.

"Commander Vincent Akano speaking, how may I help you?

"Vincent, Ezra speaking. Call me back on a secure line".

"Okay". Another momentous challenge… he really had to stop letting his anger get the best of him. He was getting too old for this job. He picked up the landline and dialed Ezra's number.

"Ezra?" Vincent asked. "Yes, it's me". He replied.

"Is there a problem?" he questioned Ezra.

"No, for a change, I've got some good news", replied Ezra.

"I could use some of that. Ropo has taken over our north compound. Vincent sadly shared.

"I know", Ezra dismally responded. "But that's enough bad news for today. Let's talk about the good news. The United States has agreed to become our allies. In approximately two hours a special surveillance team will join you. Once they assess the situation, they will help us regain control of the country".

"How in the world did that happen?" asked Vincent.

Ezra clears his throat and says, "Zara and E. got an invite to the White House through a friend of Sam Cooke's at the State Department, it turns out that the President was impressed with her.

E. says she was the consummate diplomat. She was determined not to leave until she convinced him to assist her and praise God, he did".

"Is there anything else I should know?" queried Vincent.

"No. They will brief you when they arrive. I suggest that we work with them. The sooner we do, the sooner the queen can be back on the throne. What do you think?" asked Ezra.

"Affirmative", stated Vincent.

Vincent and his team were prepared for the arrival of the Americans, who came within an hour. They ensured that the soldiers were well-fed with three proper meals each day, provided comfortable sleeping quarters, and supplied them with everything necessary to familiarize themselves with their surroundings. The moment the Queen's Army discovered that she was responsible for their much-needed assistance in securing victory during the war, a newfound sense of confidence enveloped them. She hadn't deserted them.

The Counter-Attack Begins

After a span of three days, an American agent arrived at the camp in search of his commanding officer. Going by the name Chad Niemeyer, he had been undercover as a medical practitioner in Ropo's camp doing reconnaissance. Upon submitting his report to the commander and undergoing questioning from Vincent, the team convened to finalize their strategy for moving forward.

The Special Operations Unit assigned to work with the Queen's Army was a collective force made up of Army Rangers, Special Forces (Green Berets), and Night Stalkers.

The units joined together to create a circular boundary both inside and outside of the enclosure. The Queen's Army occupied the outer perimeter, while the American Special Operations Unit took position within. The civilians were held captive in a detention camp located at the rear of the compound. Their rescue was prioritized, with all able-bodied men armed with AK-47s to support the assault. To ensure their safety, women and children were escorted into the forest.

Simultaneously, the initial attack focused on destroying the armory during nighttime. The air crackled with tension as Robo Acheampong surveyed the armory, his eyes scanning row upon row of deadly weapons. The scent of gunpowder hung heavy in the air; a foreboding reminder of the destructive potential contained within those walls. Unbeknownst to him, fate had already set its plan in motion.

As dusk settled over the horizon, a lone figure moved stealthily through the shadows, carrying a small box. Within its confines lay the catalyst for a catastrophe. Unbeknownst to the unsuspecting guards, a spark of destruction awaited its moment to ignite the inferno that would consume the armory.

Inside the armory, soldiers went about their duties, unaware of the imminent danger lurking in their midst. The arsenal, a labyrinth of weapons, ammunition, and volatile chemicals, stood as a silent testament to man's insatiable thirst for power. Little did they know that their own haven would soon turn into a crucible of destruction.

As the moon reached its zenith, a flicker of flame escaped the confines of the small box. It danced, teasing the air with its fiery embrace before finding its mark. The spark landed amidst a cache of volatile materials, igniting a chain reaction that would send shockwaves through the night.

The explosion ripped through the armory with an intensity that defied comprehension. Walls crumbled, windows shattered, and the very earth trembled beneath the onslaught. The sheer force of the blast reduced the once-proud armory to a pile of smoldering rubble, a testament to the raw power unleashed in a single, cataclysmic moment.

In the aftermath, smoke billowed from the remains of the armory, casting a haunting pall over the scene. Lieutenant Jameson emerged from the debris, his face etched with disbelief and grief. He surveyed the destruction, his heart heavy with the weight of lives lost and the realization that the armory, a symbol of safety and security, now lay in ruins.

Ropo and his troops were completely caught off guard by this surprise assault. Many of his soldiers who were not on duty at the Armory were either intoxicated or bewildered due to this unexpected turn of events, attempting to flee towards the forest but encountering resistance from Dala Dynasty Army forces.

Two hours later, control over the compound had been regained by Dala Dynasty forces, symbolized by their flag once again flying high above it. As for Ropo Acheampong himself, he found himself captured as a prisoner of war under American custody.

Later in the day, they brought him before Vincent, who had established a camp outside of the compound. There, he provided assistance to both civilians and families of soldiers. Vincent instructed them to leave him behind as he was now the responsibility of the Dala Dynasty.

He expressed gratitude for their service and encouraged them to return to their barracks for a satisfying meal and some traditional African entertainment. The soldiers humbly complied with his request.

One soldier turned to his comrade and wondered aloud, "What do you think will happen to him?" Uncertain, but aware of the devastating rumors circulating around the compound, they knew that this POW's end was near. Quick justice was the common practice of the Dala Dynasty Army, they speculated on what fate awaited him.

As the last member of the Special Forces Team boarded a helicopter, Vincent turned towards his people—the citizens he cared for—and addressed them with words that carried weight and importance.

He produced a notice that had been distributed throughout Queen Zara Akinyemi's realm during her absence - it bore her image prominently:

It stated:

$1,000,000 Bounty

for Queen Zara Akinyemi

Dead or Alive

Contact Ropo Acheampong at

234 - 10 - 777 - 4222

He stood before the people of the Dala Dynasty holding up the flyer and said the following, "Your queen, the Royal Highness was forced to flee from her own country because of this bounty that was placed on her head. She has been in hiding for the past few months because I convinced her that an exiled alive queen was better than a dead queen. The American forces that came to our aid were a result of her petitioning the American President for assistance. He said "yes" because your queen was relentless in her pursuit of an end to this foolishness. What you don't know is that this man's son attempted to rape your queen and he kidnapped her fiancé, who your king, the Honorable Oba Jaiye, selected as the man to marry his virgin daughter. Remember in the rescue mission Sarki Acheampong killed YOUR king.

Sarki Acheampong is dead, not because your former king, Oba Jaiye was an unjust man, but because he was misled by his father to think that he could be king someday". He pointed to the compound and said, "His father did all of this because he believed a lie. The Acheampongs were good people, but good people can become bad people when their lies become their truth. We all have suffered as a result of this man's idiocracy. He has sinned against his country, his queen, you, and God. You must decide his punishment today".

Almost every soldier picked up a stone that day and in a matter of moments, the threat of Ropo Acheampong was no more.

CHAPTER 7

*T*owering trees shadowed the lakefront home, their leaves ablaze with vibrant shades of red, orange, and gold. The air is crisp and invigorating, carrying the faint scent of bonfires and pumpkin spice. As the sun rose, its golden rays danced upon the tranquil waters of the lake, casting a mesmerizing reflection that added to the enchantment of this picturesque fall day. The gentle breeze rustled through the leaves, causing them to flutter and twirl in a graceful dance. A flock of geese honked overhead, their V-shaped formation adding to the natural beauty of the scene. The sound of laughter and conversation drifted from the lakefront patio, where the Alagbatas and their queen gathered to enjoy a leisurely brunch amidst the stunning autumn backdrop. The aroma of freshly brewed coffee mingled with the scent of cinnamon and nutmeg, as a warm mug was cradled in the hands of Patricia, a contented guest.

The lake shimmered like a mirror, reflecting the vibrant colors of the surrounding foliage, creating a breathtaking tapestry of nature's artistry. The sound of a distant lawnmower hummed softly, a reminder that life continued its steady rhythm even in this idyllic setting. A gentle mist rose from the lake, adding an ethereal quality to the scene. The occasional splash of a fish breaking the surface interrupted the tranquility. Patricia announced that it was time for their session and the queen reluctantly left their little paradise for another lesson.

Once they settled in the living room, Patricia asked Zara if her trip was successful. She responded, "Very!" They both rejoiced in the good news of the moment. "So", Patricia proceeded to say, "Will you be leaving us soon?"

"I'm not sure", the queen replied. "You've been such a blessing to me during my stay. I would hate to leave you when the time comes for me to return to the Dala Dynasty. But God has called me to that position and I must be obedient to his call".

"I understand", Patricia replied. "So that means that we've got to get the rest of your sessions completed ASAP. So today I wanted to talk with you about spiritual warfare. My dear protege, there are unseen spiritual forces that are assigned to work against us, especially when we decide to live for Christ. We must be prepared to fight the good fight of faith in order to prevail when we are faced with an attack from our enemy, Satan, and his imps. This battle is as real as the one in your country. When we are faced with opposition, we often look at the person whom the enemy is using to wreak havoc in our lives, but it is not the human being behind the attack, it is the spiritual force that is influencing that individual. Ephesians 6: 12 states, 'For we do not wrestle against flesh and blood, but against principalities, against powers, against the rulers of the darkness of this age, against spiritual *hosts* of wickedness in the heavenly *places*'. As a royal, you recognize your authority, but it is the people you serve who give you the permission to rule over them. Likewise, we give these demonic principalities the right to rule over us when we don't assume our rightful position in Jesus Christ and take dominion over them".

"Why are we not made aware of this in our youth?" asks Zara.

"Because the enemy of our souls is an expert in hiding things from us. He seduces us with a lie that tantalizes our flesh or puts us in a bad situation that distracts us from what's truly going on around us. He is a master deceiver".

"So how do we know what the truth is when we live in a world of lies?" Zara asks.

"You study the word of God like your life depends upon it because it does! You must renew your mind like the Bible says in Romans 12:2. That's why spiritual discipline is important. Making reading God's word one of the first things you do in the morning sets the stage for a victorious day. Knowing God's truth is liberating. We make life so hard by complicating it with our fleshly wants and desires and making them our priority when God should always come first in our lives". Patrica responds.

Zara grabs her Bible off of the coffee table. Thumbing through the pages, she asks Patricia, "Is there a guideline that will show me how to study the Bible?"

Patricia chuckles, "Yes, there are numerous books out there that can help you. Simply go to Amazon and search for one that best suits you. But Zara, please make it a priority because when the storms of life hit, you want to be ready to combat the enemy's lies with the word of God that you have stored up inside. I have a homework assignment for you. I want you to study Ephesians 6. In our next session, we will be talking about how to prepare yourself to battle the enemy".

Zara reached for her friend's hand and said, "Thank you so much Patricia for your time today. You always leave me wanting to know more about God and how I can best honor him with my life".

"You are so welcome Zara", she replied. "Now I've got to go prepare dinner for that man of mine. He is finally coming home from his mission trip".

"Oh, that's good news, Patricia. So, I assume we won't be meeting tomorrow?" Zara asked.

"Nope. I'll be here. I have a feeling you won't be here much longer, and I want to make sure that I've properly completed my assignment". she responded.

Both women embraced and bid each other goodbye. Leliah escorted Patricia to the door and handed her a big gift box wrapped with a huge red bow around it. She smiled and said, "It's your payment for this week's sessions".

Patricia reluctantly took the box and placed it in the back seat of her car, saying, "Lord, you know I don't need payment to serve you, but it's sure nice to occasionally get a beautiful gift from someone with a kind heart. Thank you!"

The Confrontation

Zara had retired to her master bedroom to contemplate her time with Patricia. The luxurious comforter started to entice her, and she soon fell asleep with an opened Bible upon her chest. Several moments later when she was just getting into the REM phase and about to embark on a journey to an imaginary castle in the air, she was startled by the brisk ringing of her telephone. Reluctantly grabbing the menacing dream interrupter, she saw that it was her mother-in-love, so she answered it.

"Hello, Julia, how are you today?" she said.

"Not so good, one of Ezra Jr.'s old girlfriends paid me a visit today and she's on her way to his office to confront him".

"What?" Zara exclaimed, suddenly popping up in the bed and knocking the Bible to the floor.

Julia went on to say, "See he was supposed to marry Penelope, but she dumped him when he ran out of money. That was over two years ago. I don't know why she is so bothered by the fact that he married you! She didn't want him".

"Julia, how long ago did she leave your house?" Zara asked.

"Well, approximately 10 minutes ago..." Julia responded.

"Thanks. Goodbye". Zara hurriedly replied.

Zara immediately ordered an Uber and changed into a hot red Dior straight dress that she was saving for a special occasion. It was one of the few designer pieces that she had in her closet here in America. It was a stunning and captivating piece of fashion that exuded confidence, elegance, and sensuality. It was the kind of garment you wore when you wanted to make a bold statement and leave a lasting impression. She coupled the dress with a pair of sexy black Christian Louboutin pumps. Zara took one last look in the mirror, satisfied with what she saw, she slipped out of the sliding glass door in her bedroom and took the stairs that led to the entrance of her home.

She timed her arrival perfectly with that of the Uber driver. He said, "Zara?"

"Yes". She responded.

"We're going to the E. Johnson Construction Company?" he asked.

"Yes," she responded. "I f you can get me to my destination quickly, I'll give you a $100 tip as part of the arrangement."

"Yes Ma'am". he responded. He put his foot on the pedal and off they went traveling at close to 80 miles per hour the whole trip.

The Old and the New Face Off

Penelope Pettai was a young millennial blonde, with flowing golden locks that cascaded down her shoulders. Her figure was perfect, a product of hours spent in the gym and careful attention to her diet. But behind her flawless appearance, there was a simmering anger and arrogance that filled her every interaction. She had been spurned by E., and it gnawed at her pride. At least she'd thought she was. He was her ace-in-the hole so to speak. She knew that she could always come back to him if she wanted to. Especially if she couldn't find a better candidate to marry her. Now he went and got married and she was pissed. She was off to his office to give him a piece of her mind. When she finished with him, he'd run to the divorce lawyer's office.

She arrived at his office a little before noon. Penelope stormed into his office past his male assistant with a putting her hand up "Talk-to-the-hand" motion. E. who was in the middle of a conversation, immediately told the person on the other end that he would call them back later and hung up.

Meanwhile, in his father's office next door, his mother had called to warn him of the impending storm called Penelope that was fast approaching their office. She couldn't get through to E. because he was on the telephone. Ezra Sr. pulled out his cellphone to record the whole thing. He would use it later to taunt his son. They were constantly playing jokes on each other in the office. He couldn't let this one pass him by. He went to E.'s doorway to get a birdseye view of the confrontation.

By that time, E. had gotten up from his desk and was approaching Penelope. She lunged at him and missed as he stepped back, the desk breaking his fall. "What the—" E. started to say, when she burst into a myriad of curse words accusing him of dumping her and marrying another woman.

Before he could respond, a flash of something human in a red dress got in between him and her and shouted "Leave my husband alone!"

Penelope was shocked by the unannounced visitor. All E. could do was watch with his mouth open in shock. Never in his life had he had two girls fighting over him, he frankly didn't know what to do, but just stood there.

Penelope shouted, "Who the hell are you?" "I am E.'s wife".

Penelope looked at E. and exclaimed, "You married a n—?"

He responded quickly while attempting to pull Zara out of the way, "Now Penelope don't insult my wife. We won't tolerate that kind of talk around here". He failed.

Zara was in warrior mode and the best he could do was wait for this all to blow over.

She looked at him and said, "I can fight my own battles, Ezra Jr.", says Zara.

With a look that would pierce the toughest armor, Zara proclaims to Penelope, "My husband is no longer interested in a relationship with you. He is happily married. Right E.?

His father, trying to save him a night on the couch looked at him and nodded up and down. "Yes, dear". He replied.

"Now you can go back to where you came from and leave us alone!" Zara shouted, pointing to the door.

Penelope's response was quick and cutting. "How dare you think you can tell me what to do. I'll slap the #!@*&% out of you". She reached her hand up to hit Zara and the grip of a galvanized steel fist circled her arm.

E. shook his head, and tried to help her when he said, "Now Penelope, I wouldn't do that if I was you—"

But before he could get the words out of his mouth, she raised her other hand and slapped Zara. Within a millisecond she was on the floor with her arm pressed behind her back. If she moved a quarter of an inch her arm would break.

"Let me go, you are hurting me", she whimpered.

Before Zara could respond the office was filled with six mighty women whose descendants were from one of the most ferocious tribes in all of Africa. Nafisa stepped forward and exclaimed "Who dare strike our queen? Today you will surely die!!!" She is about to launch forward in attack mode, and Zara looks up at her from a kneeled position and shakes her head "No." Zara released Penelope.

She slowly rose and suddenly became aware that there were five more African women in the room with their guns drawn. In a total act of surrender, she began to cry.

Zara turned to her husband, planted a sensual kiss on his lips that he didn't back down from, and said, "There's more where that came from. Come straight home tonight. You'll be glad you did".

E. responded after wiping red lipstick from his mouth, "Yes dear, gladly".

He looked at Penelope glaring at him on the floor and said, "Once you go Black, you never you never go back".

Zara and her entourage leave his office after saying goodbye to Ezra Sr. On the way to the Range Rover, Yaya asked her queen, "How did you get here?" Zara replied, "I took an Uber, of course". Nafisa and the other Alagbatas shook their heads.

Ezra Sr. stepped into E.'s office and shut the door. "Ms. Pettai, I am so sorry you had the unfortunate opportunity to meet E.'s wife in this way. She is a sweet girl. Unless of course she is provoked. Did you know she is a judo black belt?"

Silence.

"I didn't think you did", he said.

"Without any prior notice, you appeared today and behaved in a manner that would have disappointed your parents. I was acquainted with them and they were respected members of the community. Regrettably, your behavior today warranted me to contact the authorities, but due to my previous association with your parents, I refrained from doing so".

He opened the door and told his assistant, "Escort Ms. Pettai to the door". He returned to his desk without giving her a second glance.

Retaliation

The events of the previous day had settled, and E. was on the verge of uncovering the undeniable truth concealed within Willian Congreve's famous words: "A woman's fury knows no bounds when she feels scorned." He arrived at his father's office later than expected, leaving a note to explain that he would be attending a board meeting before joining him for lunch to discuss their evening plans. E. chuckled at his father's persistence in wanting grand-children from him.

If Oba Jaiye were still alive, they would have been an unstoppable team when it came to campaigning for their first grandchild.

E.'s foreman came into his office requesting his assistance on a job. He locked up his office and followed him to the worksite. One of the workers had failed to show up to work that day and the day laborer who would replace him was late. They went up on the makeshift elevator and both men went to work.

E.'s hands clutched the scaffold's railing as he worked diligently, securing bolts, and navigating the intricate web of steel beams. The construction site buzzed with activity, a symphony of machinery and voices creating a cacophony that enveloped him.

Suddenly, a disconcerting wobble ran through the scaffold. E.'s heart skipped a beat, his grip tightening instinctively. Fear seized him as he teetered on the edge, a lone figure against the expansive cityscape.

"Watch out, E.!" shouted a co-worker from below, the warning lost in the clamor of the construction site.

Desperation etched across his face, E.'s attempt to regain balance failed. The scaffold gave way beneath him, and time seemed to stretch into an agonizing slow-motion sequence. The wind roared in his ears as he plummeted, the ground rushing to meet him.

From the ground, his colleagues' cries echoed through the construction site. "Call for help! Somebody call for help!" Panic spread like wildfire among the workers as they sprinted toward the fallen scaffold.

Sirens wailed in the distance, a stark contrast to the chaos unfolding above. In those tense moments, E's name rippled through the crowd like a prayer on their lips.

As the dust settled and the sirens drew nearer, a heavy silence settled over the construction site. The reality of the accident hung in the air, a sobering reminder of the dangers inherent in their demanding work. All eyes were fixed on the aftermath, a collective hope for E's safety lingering in the air like an unspoken plea.

The Hospital Becomes Home

Zara sat on the porch, taking in the pleasant Autumn atmosphere, deep in thought about her recent conversation with Patricia. They had delved into the idea of believers being granted power through their faith, a concept that fascinated Zara. She had never realized that God intended for them to utilize this authority when facing the challenges and hardships mentioned by Jesus in John 16:33. Being a Christian leader of a dynasty, she needed to incorporate this newfound understanding into her daily responsibilities.

Just as she was about to do an extensive study on their topic of the day, the telephone rang. She put her Bible down on the lounge chair and picked up the telephone. It was unusual for anyone to call her besides

E. because she was still in hiding until all of the rebels were captured, even though their leader had met an untimely death.

"Hello, who is this?" she inquired.

"Mrs. Johnson this is Nurse Collins from Memorial Hermann hospital. Unfortunately, your husband has been in a serious workplace accident. When can you get here?"

Zara's heart skipped a beat. She forced herself not to let her emotions take over. Her husband needed her.

"We live off of 3186, how far are you from here?" Zara asked.

The nurse responded, "Our address is 920 Frostwood Dr, Houston, TX 77024. Unfortunately, according to Google Maps, that's a little over an hour and a half away from you".

"Do you have a helipad?" the queen inquired.

"Yes, but ma'am you need—" she replied, but Zara purposefully interrupted her and said, "Please tell the doctor, I'll be there soon. Thank you". She hung up and called the air charter service. Within ten minutes, she and Nafisa were boarding a helicopter to the hospital. The other women would meet them there within the next few hours because they were traveling by SUV. While in the air she texted Ezra Sr. and he promised to meet her at the hospital. She also alerted him of the fact that she was about to break the law, by landing on the helipad at Memorial Hermann. He texted back, "Don't worry about it. It will be handled".

Ezra Sr. told the members of the board that his son had been in a critical accident and he was needed at the hospital. He turned to one of his board members and said, "Henry, you're also on the board at Memorial Hermann, aren't you?"

He replied, "Yes".

"My daughter-in-law is arriving at the hospital by helicopter. Can you see that she doesn't have any trouble with security? She's a royal and a personal friend of the President's". There was a loud gasp in the room from one of the board members.

Henry nodded.

"Thank you very much. Expect a box of your favorite Scotch on your desk in the morning". Ezra said.

"It's not necessary, just take care of your family". Henry quickly responded.

Ezra sent him a genuine look of sincere appreciation.

He turned to his assistant and said, "Denise, get me a car pronto".

"It's already waiting for you downstairs sir. I 'll be praying for Ezra Jr.", she said.

"Thank you", he replied as he made his way to the elevator. The elevator doors opened, and he was grateful that it was empty. Ezra immediately started petitioning God for his only son's life.

CHAPTER 8

When she got there, the two hospital security officers met Zara at the helipad. "Are you Queen Zara Akinyemi Johnson?" he said.

"Yes, I am", she replied.

"We have been instructed to accompany you to your husband's hospital room, ma'am. Is this woman a member of your husband's family?" he said.

"She is my bodyguard who accompanies me wherever I go", Zara responded.

He looked at the man beside him and he said, "Let her go with her. Mrs. Johnson, I am Captain Reynolds. I am in charge of security here at the hospital. If you need any assistance, please don't hesitate to call me. Here's my card".

Zara responded, "Thank you, Captain Reynolds. Your kindness is appreciated. Now where is my husband, he needs me".

"Right this way ma'am". The two gentlemen escorted Zara and Nafisa to a private room in the ICU unit.

In this particular room on the fifth floor of Memorial Hermann Hospital Ezra Johnson Jr. was valiantly fighting for his very existence. Within the sterile confines of the hospital room, he lay motionless on a meticulously made hospital bed, his weakened muscular body intricately intertwined with an array of life-sustaining machines and monitors. These technological marvels, with their blinking lights and intricate wiring, serve as a lifeline, monitoring every vital sign and providing the necessary support to keep his existence intact. The rhythmic beeping of the heart monitor echoed through the room, a constant reminder of the delicate balance between life and death. The atmosphere was heavy with a sense of urgency and hope, as the dedicated medical team tirelessly worked to ensure E.'s well- being. The room was filled with an amalgamation of sounds - the soft hum of the ventilator, the gentle whirring of the infusion pump, and the occasional rustling of the medical staff as they tended to his needs. The air was permeated with the distinct scent of antiseptic, a reminder of the sterile environment that is crucial in preventing any potential infections.

Every movement, every breath, was carefully monitored and analyzed, as the medical professionals strived to decipher the intricate puzzle that was E.'s health. Time seemed to stand still within the confines of the ICU, as the battle for life waged on. It is in this solemn and yet hopeful setting that the true resilience of the human spirit was revealed, as E. fought against all odds, refusing to succumb to the clutches of death. The ICU became a microcosm of life itself, where the fragility of existence was juxtaposed with the unwavering determination to survive.

At first glimpse, he looked like he was simply asleep, but after further inspection, Zara realized that this indeed was her husband, and he was fighting for his life. Before anyone realized it, the queen of the Dala Dynasty had gracefully slid down the wall of her husband's room and melted on the floor in a puddle of human flesh. Incognizant of her surroundings, searching for a place where the possibility of living life without him wouldn't utterly destroy her.

After regaining consciousness, Zara found herself enveloped in the scent of ammonia, cradled by her father-in-law. Initially, she mistook him for her beloved partner, but as her sight sharpened, she recognized that he was an older version.

Minutes earlier, Ezra Sr. walked into his son's room and witnessed the doctors and nurses trying to resuscitate Zara. He bellowed out in a sharp commanding voice, "What in the world are you all doing to my children? Step aside he ordered". He picked Zara up off the floor like she was a broken doll and took her over to the sofa and sat there commanding the medical staff to bring smelling salts. Reprimanding them for not being more sensitive, meanwhile accessing the status of his son. He identified the doctor in charge and began drilling him on his son's condition.

He turned her care over to Nafisa and he asked the doctor to meet him out in the hallway.

"Sir, I didn't get your name", Ezra Sr. said to the doctor.

"I 'm Doctor Frank Ebai, the head Neurosurgeon here at Memorial Hermann".

"Dr. Ebai, please accept my sincere apologies, but when I walked in all I saw was utter chaos. I hope you can sympathize. My son surrounded by all of those machines and my daughter-in-love passed out on the floor was a bit much for an old man like me", he humbly petitioned.

"I understand", he responded.

So, what's the real prognosis doctor?" Ezra Sr. asked.

"Frankly, I've told you all I can. We are currently running tests to determine the severity of his injuries. What we do know is that he is in the best hospital in the city with some of the best head trauma specialists in the nation". he reached out and patted Ezra Sr.'s shoulder saying, "Mr. Johnson, if your son survives the night, there is a good chance that he's going to make it".

"But what if he doesn't?," replies Ezra Sr.

"Let's just wait and see what happens. He's in great physical shape and it appears as though he has a lot to live for. All we can do is wait until morning". said the doctor.

Ezra Sr., says, "We will definitely wait. Doctor, are you a praying man?"

"Yes, I am." Dr. Ebai responded.

Ezra shook his head and said, "Then that gives me some additional comfort".

He walked away to go give his ex-wife Julia a call wondering, if Zara fainted, what in the world would Julia do when she saw him?

Death, You Have No Sting

The good news was that E. made it through the night. The bad news was that he had slipped into a coma in the middle of the night as a result of his head injury. Zara stopped crying around midnight and just sat by his bed continuously praying to God for the complete healing of her husband. It was she who noticed that he was unresponsive and called in the night nurse who immediately called Dr. Ebai. Her suspicions were confirmed when he gave her an updated prognosis. He assured her that this wasn't the worst thing that could happen, but in a situation like this, all they could do was wait and pray.

Julia showed up at 10:00 a.m. Immediately she went to her son's bedside kissed his forehead and hugged Zara.

She, Curtis, and the children were on a family vacation in Orlando Florida at Disneyland when she got the news. She'd caught the first available flight out and was too tired to do anything but stand in agreement in prayer with Zara for her son's healing. She was so exhausted after a day at the park with her children and the unexpected flight, that she fell asleep on the couch without even knowing it. Ezra Sr.'s concerns were unwarranted.

Nafisa was in the family waiting room awaiting further instructions from Zara when Hiba came to relieve her. She checked in on her queen and brought her a change of clothes. Zara would not leave E's side for anyone other than the medical professionals who came to care for him. It wasn't until Patricia showed up unexpectedly that Zara went to join her in the family waiting room.

To her surprise, there was a tall elderly man in his early 70's with salt and pepper gray hair and a bushy mustache sitting beside her holding her hand. Patricia greeted her with a hug and Zara stayed as long as was proper in the arms of her mentor. The two women reluctantly released each other, and Patrcia turned to the elderly gentleman beside her.

"Queen Zara, this is my husband Jim. Jim this is my beautiful friend I was telling you about", she said.

He extended his hand and said, "Pleased to meet you, Queen Zara. I am so sorry to hear about your husband. Is there anything we can do?"

"Would you mind offering a prayer for him? His room is just down the hallway. I have faith that God has the power to do anything, but I'm still learning about the practice of prayer. In my reading, I came across a passage in the Bible that says when two or more people gather in God's name, He manifests His presence. It would mean so much to me if you could join me in lifting up this request through prayer," she earnestly requested.

"Of course we will. Just lead the way", He turned to his wife and said, "Honeybunch, you got your oil with you?"

"Always!" she responded.

He grabbed Zara's arm and said, "Well Queen Zara we're ready".

The trio entered the room and Dr. Ebai was just leaving to complete his rounds.

Patricia said, "Glory to God, your husband has risen Zara! Pleased to meet you Zara's husband. Wow, when God does something, he does it quickly".

Jim and Zara look at each other confused. Dr. Ebai was quick to straighten out the matter. "No, no, I'm not Mrs. Johnson's husband. I'm her husband's doctor, Frank Ebai. Mr. Johnson is over there". He turned and pointed toward the hospital bed behind him.

All eyes went to where E. was resting quietly with his mother Julia standing beside him.

"Jesus!" Patricia said, "Zara, I thought you were married to a Mandingo, but you're married to an Adonis".

"Now honeybunch apologize to these nice people, they are going through enough right now without you insulting them", Jim responded.

Dr. Ebai was trying hard to keep up a professional front but expediently excused himself from the room under the guise of completing his rounds.

Zara responded, "She's fine Jim. Patricia has never met my husband before because he's usually at work when she comes for a visit. This is my mother-in-love, Julia. Julia this is Patricia the lady I was telling you about who has been teaching me about the Bible".

"Pleased to meet you", she acknowledged the new guests saying, "This is my son Ezra Jr., Zara's real husband".

Everyone laughed.

Jim detached himself from the group and walked up to E.'s bed curiously examining him. "What did you say his name was?"

She replied, "Ezra Johnson Jr."

Is his grandfather, Moses Johnson, a fella who was a missionary? Matter of fact his whole family were missionaries until his son started doing construction".

"Yes, that's my ex-husband's father. Did you know him?"

Absolutely! He's the reason I'm a missionary today.

Patricia exclaimed, "What?"

"Yes honeybunch", he said, "Those Johnson boys got called to the ministry early and took the Great

Commission seriously. They started going all over the world telling people about Jesus. He had three other brothers and they all died on the mission field, most of them went to Africa".

Zara asked, "How did you meet my husband's grandfather?

Jim replied, "He came to our church one time. Back in the day churches used to adopt missionaries and send them financial support. He was one of the missionaries we supported. I was about nine years old when I met him. His testimony compelled me to accept Jesus Christ as my Lord and Saviour".

"Look at God", Patricia whispered.

"It would be my honor to pray for your husband Queen Zara", Jim said. "But, let me tell you something, God has already healed him. The Johnson boys and Jesus are in heaven already petitioning our Heavenly Father for his life. It ain't time for him to go to heaven yet. That boy has work to do. Don't count it strange that the enemy has tried to take him out three times. He's afraid of what's in him".

Julia started to weep.

He turned to Zara and said, "God says, don't count it strange that you married a man from another ethnic background and lineage. He planned it that way because of what he has placed in you and what's in him. You are the ruler of a small country that will have a major impact on the world for Christ. You were born to be his wife, and he was born to be your husband before your fathers even made a blood covenant on that holy hill in Africa. You and your seed have been commissioned to continuously point the world to Jesus Christ until his second coming. You have been strategically placed on the throne for such a time as this and Ezra, whose name means helper, which was derived from the Hebrew name, "Azaryahu", which means "God helps" has been purposely placed beside you as a man who rests in the authority of God. He is your spiritual helpmeet, and he WILL live to help you fulfill this mandate".

He turned to his wife and said, "Honeybunch, give me the oil". Patricia immediately responded and Jim placed his hand on E.'s head saying, "I decree and declare that the Satanic attack against this family ceases today.

In the authority invested in me in the name of Jesus Christ, I command Satan to lose their destiny right now! I also decree that everything, and I mean everything that has been stolen from this young couple will be restored 100-fold. I speak to you Ezra Johnson Jr. as Jesus the living Christ did to Lazarus when he was in the tomb, in his mighty name, come forth!"

When Jim looked up from his prayer, his wife was praying in the Holy Spirit, Queen Zara was prostrate on the floor, and Julia was weeping like a baby. He shook his head, thinking, "These women love themselves some Jesus".

The Investigation

The scaffold incident made the 5:00 pm news the evening before. Ezra received numerous telephone calls, texts, and emails inquiring about his son's health and his conference room was full of flowers and condolences from his customers, board members, and close friends. He forwarded everything to his assistant, she was more than capable of handling this situation. He had other more important things to do, especially this morning. He was to meet the safety inspector at the site which had been closed since the accident. When he arrived, the police were there also.

"Good morning Mr. Johnson". said the inspector. "This is Officer Lopez from the Houston Police Department's Homicide Division".

"Good morning, Paul, Officer Lopez, I 'm confused, did someone die that I didn't know about?" Ezra said.

Paul responded, "No sir, but when I inspected the accident site the other day, I found this in the rubble". He hands Ezra Sr. a frayed rope. "This rope was cut before the scaffold broke".

"Is there any way to determine if the rope was cut by a metal object when the scaffold collapsed?" asked Ezra Sr.

"Indeed, that is a possibility. However, based on the angle at which the rope was severed, it is highly unlikely that it occurred during the fall". Paul said.

"So what makes you think it was a deliberate attempt to end my son's life?" asked Ezra Sr.

"The frayed edges on this side of the rope don't match the rope on the other side. See this rope has a cleaner break than the other", responded Paul.

"I see", said Ezra. "So, Officer Lopez, what's our next step?"

"I 've assigned an officer to your son's hospital room just in case the killer attempts to finish the job. We'll also need to interview everybody who was on the worksite that day. Was there anyone who had a beef with your son, any of the workers, customers, an ex-wife?" the officer said.

"Unfortunately, that's a long story, but recently, an ex-girlfriend of his came by the office and caused quite a scene because he'd gotten married", he responded.

"What's her name?" asked the officer.

"Penelope Pettai. My assistant would have her contact information. She was engaged to marry my son at one time".

"I see. I will also need to interview you". said the officer.

"Fine. I need to run by the hospital to check on my son. Can we meet at lunchtime in my office?" asked Ezra Sr.

"Sure". the officer responded.

"Paul, thank you for doing a thorough investigation", said Ezra Sr.

"It's my job, Mr. Johnson". he replied.

"Have a nice day gentlemen", said Ezra Sr. "I'll see you later today Officer Lopez."

"Yes sir". he responded.

Ezra Sr. got in the town car, and his driver asked, "Where to Mr. Johnson?"

"The hospital" he replied. In the heart of the city, amidst the chaos of rush hour traffic, the sleek black town car glided down the crowded freeway. Its polished exterior gleamed under the radiant city lights, exuding an air of elegance and sophistication. The rhythmic purr of the engine and the gentle hum of the tires on the pavement provided a soothing soundtrack to the urban symphony.

As the town car weaved through lanes with effortless grace, Ezra Sr.'s mind drifted to a time long past. Memories of his son's earlier days flooded his thoughts. He was torn between his regrets from the past and the joy he'd had watching his son become the man he was today. Children weren't supposed to die before their parents. Ezra Sr. couldn't imagine a world without his son. He closed his eyes laid his head back on the seat and prayed, "God please let my son live, I need him".

CONCLUSION

As the morning light seeped through the hospital room window, E. slowly regained consciousness. His eyes fluttered open, adjusting to the brightness. The sterile smell of the hospital invaded his senses, and he could hear the low hum of medical equipment in the background.

Turning his head to the side, he saw his wife, Zara, curled up in a chair beside his bed, fast asleep. Her chest rose and fell rhythmically, her peaceful expression belying the worry lines that had etched themselves on her face during his time in a coma.

Ezra's heart swelled with gratitude as he took in the sight of his devoted partner. The journey to recovery had been arduous, but he knew he had never been alone.

Zara had been by his side every step of the way, offering unwavering support and love.

He reached out a trembling hand, gently brushing a lock of hair away from Zara's face. Her eyelids fluttered, and she slowly stirred, blinking away the remnants of sleep. As her eyes focused on E., they widened in surprise and delight.

"E.!" she exclaimed, her voice filled with a mixture of relief and joy. "You're awake!"

A smile tugged at the corners of E.'s lips as he nodded weakly. "Yes, Zara. I'm awake."

Tears welled up in Zara's eyes as she leaned over, pressing a tender kiss to E.'s forehead. "Oh, thank God," she whispered, her voice choked with emotion.

They held each other's gaze, their love and gratitude flowing between them like an unbreakable bond. At that moment, all the hardships they had endured seemed insignificant compared to the strength of their connection.

As the medical staff rushed in to assess E.'s condition, Zara remained by his side, never once leaving his line of sight. Together, they faced the challenges that lay ahead, knowing that as long as they had each other, they could overcome anything.

Their love had weathered the storm of E.'s coma, and now it would carry them forward, into a future filled with renewed hope and endless possibilities.

Back at the Office

During lunchtime at a construction site, the atmosphere came alive with the sound of clinking tools and laughter. The construction workers at E. Johnson and Son Construction were like any other construction company, they all gathered in groups, finding a spot to sit and enjoy their well-deserved break. Some brought their lunches, while others ordered food from nearby food trucks. The air was filled with the aroma of various cuisines, ranging from sandwiches and salads to hot meals. The workers engaged in lively conversations, sharing stories and jokes, and building camaraderie.

They discussed the progress of the project, exchanging tips and tricks they'd learned along the way when the topic turned to the happenings in the main office. This particular day the Johnson's assistant joined the lunchtime conversation.

"Pettai, your sister came by the office the other day and gave E. some serious grief", the assistant said.

"What you mean, Jersey? I heard it was the other way around. She had a right to be pissed,

E. promised to marry her and then he goes off and marries someone else". he adamantly claimed.

Jersey responded, "No man, she came storming into the office and pushed him up against the desk. That's how mad she was. And when his wife showed up, she got worse, she tried to slap her twice. E.'s wifey knows judo so she floored her".

The workers in attendance responded with some loud boisterous exclamations, expressing their surprise, disbelief, and excitement. Some exclaimed "What' s happening? E.'s married? So that's where he went for that two weeks.", while others commented, "Is this for real?" One worker even expressed regret at missing the event, saying "I wish I had been there to witness that!" Another worker even stood up screaming "I love girl fights, tell me more Jersey!"

Pettai's embarrassment was the size of Texas. He stammered, "Man stop making up stories. You know my sister wouldn't hurt a fly. She's all talk. I do her fighting for her".

"That's the problem man". a voice said from the back of the crowd that had gathered around them.

Pettai shouted, "Who said that? Come say that to my face!

The voice replied, "See what I mean. Man, when it comes to your sister you ain't got no damn

sense. You believe everything she says. Her mouth ain't no prayer book. I've seen her on the prowl before and she is ruthless".

Pettai shouted louder this time, "You've got a big mouth man? You don't even know my sister?

In the midst of this lively scene, stepping out of the crowd, a large-sized Portuguese construction worker stood tall and broad-shouldered, exuding strength and confidence. His rugged features were complemented by a well-groomed beard, which added to his rugged charm. The sight of him commanded attention, as his presence alone spoke volumes about his capabilities. With a determined look in his eyes, he stepped forward, ready to face any challenge that came his way.

Someone from the crowd shouted, "Don't kill him, Fabio!"

"Man, I KNOW your sister in ways that you can't even imagine". He leaned forward and whispered into Pettai's ear, "I saw you the morning of E', s accident on site before anyone got to work. Now do you really want to challenge me in front of these fellows?"

Pettai backed away and turned toward Jersey saying, "Man you started all this. I ought to whip your #!@*&% instead…"

"I wouldn't try that if I were you", a voice of authority said from outside the crowd. Ezra Sr. was standing there with Officer Lopez. "You men get back to work. Lunchtime is over!" Pettai, I'll see you in my office in 5. Officer Lopez and I would like to have a conversation with you".

Wearing a false display of confidence, he retorted, "Of course, boss."

Fabio leaned in again, whispering into Pettai's ear, "Do the right thing, or I will".

That afternoon another God-sized miracle took place, Robert Pettai confessed to the attempted murder of Ezra Johnson Jr. after he saw the video of his sister's visit.

Soon after, Ezra Sr. got the telephone call that his son was awake and very much alive. He laid his head down on his desk and cried tears of gratitude.

EPILOGUE

*V*incent was filled with immense happiness upon receiving the news that Queen Zara and Prince Ezra would be returning to the Dala Dynasty in just one week. The entire Palace Compound was undergoing a thorough restoration in preparation for their arrival.

In the previous week, Queen Zara conducted a live broadcast from the office of the United States President. During this momentous event, they officially signed a treaty between their respective countries, which was subsequently broadcasted throughout the dynasty. Addressing her people directly, she spoke these words:

Ladies and gentlemen, esteemed guests, and fellow citizens of our beloved nation, Today marks a historic moment in our country's journey towards progress, unity, and prosperity. As I stand before you, a returning exiled African queen, my heart overflows with love, admiration, and gratitude for each one of you. It is an honor to be welcomed back to the land that has always held a special place in my soul.

For months, I have yearned for this day, a day when I can express my unwavering love for our country and its extraordinary citizens. Throughout my exile, my heartbeat in synchrony with the pulse of our nation, never forgetting the struggles and resilience that define our people. I have carried our culture, our traditions, and our hopes in every step I took, every word I spoke, and every decision I made.

Today, I stand before you not only as a queen but also as a symbol of a new alliance, a partnership that holds immense potential for the future of our great nation. The United States of America, with its rich history and unwavering support for freedom and democracy, has extended its hand in friendship and collaboration. This alliance signifies an opportunity for us to join hands with a global powerhouse, learn from their successes, and forge a brighter future together.

But let us not forget that our strength lies within ourselves, within the love we carry for our homeland, and within the power of unity.

Our country is a tapestry woven with the threads of diverse cultures, languages, and traditions. It is this diversity that makes us unique, that enriches our collective identity, and that fuels our progress.

As we embark on this new chapter, let us remember the lessons of our past. Let us learn from the mistakes and challenges that have shaped us. Let us embrace the spirit of collaboration, dialogue, and understanding that will guide us towards a brighter future. Together, we can overcome any obstacle, build a society that upholds justice and equality, and create opportunities for every citizen to thrive.

My fellow citizens, today I stand before you not just as your queen, but as a servant of the people. My love for this nation knows no bounds, and my commitment to its citizens is unwavering. I pledge to dedicate myself to the betterment of our society, to champion the rights of the marginalized, and to foster an environment where every individual has the opportunity to succeed.

In this new alliance with the United States, let us be guided by the principles of mutual respect, shared goals, and a commitment to the well-being of our people. Together, we can build bridges of understanding, foster economic growth, and create a future where our children can thrive.

I stand here today, humbled, and grateful, ready to embark on this journey with each one of you. Let us join hands, my fellow citizens, and together, let us create a legacy that will be remembered for generations to come.

Thank you, and may God bless our beloved nation.

BIOGRAPHICAL NOTE

Sharon C. Jenkins' novels explores miracles, enduring love, and the strength of an unquenchable faith, taking readers from American streets to an African kingdom, and leaving them with renewed hope and belief in love's triumph.

Learn more about Sharon at:

www.theliterarymidwifeunlimited.com or

www.superauthorgranny.com

Notes

Notes

Notes

Notes

REFERENCES

Collins, W. (2019). *A Warrior's Sword.* WestBow Press.

Nelson, T. (1982). *Holy Bible: The New King James Version.* T. Nelson.

Sharon Carter Jenkins, & Balonwu, P. (2023). *The Untold Love Story.* The Master Communicator's Writing Services.

It all began in *The Untold Love Story,* Book One in The Virtuous Woman Book Series. Get your copy at any major digital bookstore TODAY!

www.ingramcontent.com/pod-product-compliance
Lightning Source LLC
Chambersburg PA
CBHW040802120726
48005CB00012B/1274